THE GARDENS
OF CONSOLATION

Parisa Reza

THE GARDENS
OF CONSOLATION

*Translated from the French
by Adriana Hunter*

Europa
editions

Reza

Europa Editions
214 West 29th Street
New York, N.Y. 10001
www.europaeditions.com
info@europaeditions.com

Copyright © 2015 by Editions Gallimard, Paris
First Publication 2016 by Europa Editions

Translation by Adriana Hunter
Original title: *Les jardins de consolation*
Translation copyright © 2016 by Europa Editions

Library of Congress Cataloging in Publication Data is available
ISBN 978-1-60945-350-3

Reza, Parisa
The Gardens of Consolation

Book design by Emanuele Ragnisco
www.mekkanografici.com

Cover photo © SanerG/iStock

Prepress by Grafica Punto Print – Rome

Printed in the USA

CONTENTS

THE GARDENS
OF CONSOLATION

I
HAVVA,
THE INNOCENCE OF HELL

To the east, bare earth, as far as the eye can see. To the west, hills, in places crumpled as a camel's hide, in others smooth as a woman's breast. Then on the horizon, mountains. And a road, traced along the length of the desert, the length of the mountains, from Isfahan to Tehran. Perhaps this road sets off from further away, from somewhere in the south of Iran. Perhaps it begins beside the sea, at Bouchehr. But for Talla, the world does not reach beyond Isfahan and Tehran. Tehran and Isfahan are the most extreme limits she has heard mentioned, the last outposts before oblivion. Beyond that would be home to djinns and peris, will-o'-the-wisps and ogres. Not that this means she can situate the two cities in relation to each other, or even attribute them with any form or substance. They are merely necessary words to shape the world. Tehran, Isfahan, and, between the two, Kashan. And Mecca, the counterweight to the pagan world, holding within its walls the antidote to all the vice and suffering of man, man who is constantly led astray by bewitching creatures lurking in the bowels of the earth. There should be a bridge connecting her world to Mecca, which she pictures suspended in space, hovering over everything. And little more than that.

Talla is traveling this road, riding a donkey, and her husband Sardar walks beside her. No other living creature travels with them. Alone like this, Sardar is afraid of bandits, and Talla of ogres. But they are carried by their faith, for the void contains only God, and the line traced by this road, only man's endless footfalls.

In this year 1299 of the Iranian calendar, Talla is twelve. Three days earlier she left her village, Ghamsar, for the first time.

According to its inhabitants, Ghamsar is a lost corner of paradise fallen from heaven. Ghamsar is ringed by mountains and home to a handful of families whose artistry and workmanship are feted all over the East. For this is where the purest, most fragrant rosewater is made. The rosewater used to perfume Mecca itself.

In Ghamsar, at the gates of hell and the source of paradise, blooms Mohamed's flower; it is here, in this village, to the west of the scorching desert of the Iranian plateau, that the Persian rose grows.

It is no coincidence that paradise was born in the desert. No creature surrounded by greenery could have imagined its glories. When locals say Ghamsar is a paradise, they recognize it as an improbable object of desire: a garden of flowers and fruit.

Here, the red flower blooms among vines, amid trees of hazelnuts, almonds, cherries, peaches . . . Here, the river finds its source in the mountains, runs through the village, irrigates the plantations, and never runs dry. Here, people can bathe their whole bodies in limpid pools, or tirelessly drink the pure water as it springs from the ground and flows in peaceful rivulets. At Ghamsar the wind does not raise dust but spreads the smell of roses, a gift from God, the flower of Mohamed. Here, nightingales sing.

In Ghamsar, the art of making rosewater is passed from one generation to the next by a scant hundred men and women. At the end of every spring, at dawn, before the sun's first rays have spoiled the flowers' fragrance, they pick hundreds of pounds of petals and make their precious essence in sufficient quality and quantity to satisfy and honor Iran, as well as Arabia and India, to the west and east. They know that this essence is prized far away, far, far away. But for most of them, the world actually ends twenty miles to the east, in Kashan. In rose season a cara- van laden with rosewater travels there with great ceremony. The rest of the year the men go there regularly to sell fruit and veg- etables, their surplus produce, and to buy the simplest necessi- ties: sugar, tea, salt, pepper, and tobacco. Occasionally, a few venture as far as Tehran or Isfahan; some never return, others reappear one day like a mirage, exhausted by their travels.

The women, though, never leave the village. To them, the mountains have only one face, the one they see with their own eyes. The other face exists only in fables about the adventures and loves of princes and kings who confront giants, ogres, and dragons.

Talla has never been beyond the mountains. And yet her reclusive life felt enormous to her. She worked in the orchards, picked roses in spring, fed and slaughtered hens, milked ewes and made butter, cheese, and yogurt. She believed in all the legends people told, in djinns and peris, in curses and talis- mans. But what truly delighted Talla was climbing to the tops of trees, swimming in fresh water, running across the plains, and hollering across the mountains.

They left Ghamsar at dawn on the track that runs along the foot of Mount Ashke.[1] Once out of the mountains, Talla saw a vast desert of red sand before her.

She can now associate the word desert with its reality. A fascinating reality. They make slow progress. The donkey's hooves sink into the sand, slowing its pace. The sun is already up, the kindly rays of mid-fall spare them any crushing heat. Talla thinks she is in a dream, in the middle of nowhere. But Sardar speaks softly to her. He has already experienced this terror, this lost feeling, so he reassures, gives hope.

"When we arrive, when we reach the place you can't yet see, there will be life again, and water and greenery and a secure future."

Talla looks off into the distance, but the glaring light of the desert masks the view. Dazzled, she appeals to heaven and endlessly recites verses from the Koran. Does she know that the desert prophesy lies in this same light, this very silence? Does she know the desert kills or toughens those who cross it?

Several times Talla thinks she sees an oasis. She points it out to Sardar, who explains about mirages: evil creatures that trick travelers from one illusion to the next, luring them toward the wastelands from which no one ever returns. Talla shudders at the thought of invisible malevolent creatures marauding around her, and does not stop praying the whole time it takes them to cross those sands.

[1] The word means "tear" in Persian.

The day trickles by with her in this same state: half wonderment, half torment. They arrive on the outskirts of Kashan at sunset, and spend the night in a caravansery. A ruin. A few walls, barely still standing, whose only purpose is to mark out a space in which men and animals sleep side by side. What matters is for the donkey to eat, drink, and rest. Sardar and Talla settle in a corner well away from the camels and their owners. They spread a length of cloth on the ground, eat some bread and cheese, and lie down next to each other. Talla looks at the sky, the intricate lace gilded with stars that she is used to seeing overhead every night and that can be viewed this clearly from only two places on earth, this being one of them. But the geographical characteristics and the astronomical visibility of the place matter little to Talla; she is an inherent part of the natural world and its manifestations—and these include the sky, be it immaculately blue or starry black. And she falls asleep.

For three days now, Talla has been gazing at the road. Fascinated by this long line she must tread without ever straying.

She was so gripped by Kashan's beauty and all the fantastical things it had to offer, she almost fell into a swoon, but soon found it hard to cope with this surfeit of new sights. What a relief it was leaving the town behind and returning to the calm of the desert. She is still afraid of meeting beasts and monsters, though.

"Which hole in the ground will they emerge from?"

Neither the donkey's regular hoofbeats on the earth beaten by successive caravans nor Sardar's monotonous voice talking constantly to reassure her succeed in disturbing the silence of the desert. A great emptiness absorbing them, indifferent to their passage. Talla is numbed by it.

As she snoozes she becomes obscurely aware of a sound. She strains forward on the donkey's back and peers into the distance. The noise grows louder and suddenly rips through the peace of the desert. The source of the sound is hiding behind a cloud of dust, heading straight for her. The monster finally appears, a black headless hulk with bulging eyes set into its body, its round feet powering toward her at inconceivable speed, its mouth exhaling a horrifying scream. Her every ancestor's every nightmare instantly leaps to life in her mind. But at the last moment her survival instinct gets the better of her terror, and she jumps from the donkey and runs away, shrieking in horror and calling on all the saints for help.

Sardar is astonished to see his wife leap from the donkey with the agility of a tiger, and he takes a moment to realize Talla has never seen a car before. He has a lot of trouble calming her and persuading her to remount the donkey. How to explain cars to her? He himself took a while accepting that such contraptions could exist even though he did not understand how.

"We don't need to understand everything," he says. "If we had to stop every time we came across something new in a big city, we would travel as slowly as a tortoise. You just get used to it."

As for the passengers in the passing Renault, Talla's panic certainly made them laugh; they were quick to relate the anecdote when they arrived, roaring with laughter all over again. They were so used to the contraption they thought they had invented it.

Sardar is twenty this year. Three years earlier, after his father died and his inheritance was shared out with his three brothers, he called on his uncle and asked him to climb up the hill with him. This is where men go to discuss important matters. They climbed the hill side by side in silence, and at the top, overlooking all of Ghamsar, they could see the roofs of houses scattered among the orchards, as well as the river, the plantations, women's colorful scarves, flocks of sheep, and a few donkeys. Here Sardar turned to face his uncle, head lowered in deference to his elder, and told him he was leaving for Tehran, for good. Not saying whether he was seeking adventure or fortune. Then he asked whether his uncle would like to buy his land and his rifle. His uncle thought for a moment, then offered him five tomans for the lot, there and then. He did not try to hold his nephew back. Virtually no one ever sells land in Ghamsar; plots are handed from father to son and stay in the family. This was a godsend. Sardar was making a poor deal but a man cannot barter with his own uncle; uncles are owed respect and consideration, particularly as, since Sardar's father had died, this uncle had become head of the family. Sardar's land should stay in the family. Selling it to someone else at a better price would have been a betrayal. Sardar agreed, although he thought privately that his rifle alone was worth five tomans. And, on that same hill, he promised himself he would make a fortune with his five tomans so that word of this would one day reach his uncle's ears.

Sardar wanted to leave at any cost. He wanted to leave because he believed—no, he could feel—that this land was becoming cursed. Too many envious eyes had been cast over it. The outsiders who sometimes came to stay in Ghamsar, the dignitaries from Kashan who had built houses to enjoy the mild climate in summer or the isolation, far from the world, in the tranquility of their gardens, or even the traders from Kashan who sometimes came to sell their wares here; they must all have cast a spell on Ghamsar.

In less than fifty years, in his father's and grandfather's life-time, Ghamsar had endured cholera, then an earthquake that destroyed everything. Death upon death . . . And in his own lifetime, famine. It was when he was nine, he remembers people selling off their land for a few zucchini, remembers being hungry, eating tree roots and meat from dead animals, remembers his mother dying in pregnancy, exhausted, and this on land that can provide a profusion of delectable foods. She died in this corner of paradise, so powerful was the curse.

And now pillagers, bandits, and Mashallah Khan Kashi's gang appeared out of nowhere taking everything in their path. People fled into the mountains and came home to find only desolation.

The evil eye. Ghamsar was too beautiful for the jealous desert people to leave it in peace. Sardar could feel it: If he stayed here he would perish. He did not know when or how, but he felt quite sure of it.

Once the sale of his land was concluded, Sardar approached his uncle on a supremely important point: He asked him for Talla's hand. The girl with the green eyes from the upper end of the village, the girl for whom his heart beat. He wanted Ghamsari blood to flow in his children's veins, and told his uncle so. Sardar had often watched his chosen one: She would make a good wife, for she was hardworking. She came and went with conviction and no childish dallying. And beautiful, too, with her emerald eyes, tall and slender, a very pink little mouth, and two braids falling down to her waist from beneath her scarf. He did not intend to take her with him, but meant to leave her in Ghamsar while he found himself a position in Tehran, and then he would come for her. He did not know Tehran, nor the road there; it would be wiser not to involve Talla in this hazardous adventure straightaway. But his heart was instructing him to marry her before traveling so far afield. He knew he needed to be married to Talla in order to accomplish great things, he needed her to be waiting for him.

As a general rule, the people from the upper village and the lower village in Ghamsar lived in peace alongside each other; nevertheless, they did not mix, choosing to keep their distance. Depending on which part of the village they came from, people's lives were not altogether the same, and neither were their dreams. The lower village was on the way out of Ghamsar, and its inhabitants were more outward-looking, more influenced by the outside world. Had Sardar lived in the upper village, he might not have had such a strong desire to leave. But the route to the wider world was on this side, it called to people, lured them; some took it and others did not, but all inevitably contemplated it.

Talla's father thought this young man from the lower village who had the courage to travel far was honoring his family. That is what he said. Truth be told, what struck him most was that Sardar was a nephew of the new head of the clan in the lower village. Good alliances should never be turned down, and daughters were a way of sealing them. That was their primary value. Beyond that, whether they stayed or left mattered little.

Out of respect for customary propriety, Talla's father took some time to reflect and to discuss the matter with the mullah, then he granted Sardar Talla's hand. Having agreed they could be married, he said the marriage should not be celebrated or consummated until Sardar's return. If Sardar met with misfortune, if he did not return, Talla's father wanted to have no trouble in finding another husband for his daughter. Her innocence must be preserved.

And so, at the age of nine, Talla was married, and proud to be so. She liked the look of her husband, he was a tall young man with wide shoulders and a fine bearing. He had a luminous face and was a good man, she knew it.

The couple did not speak to each other until the day Sardar left. In the meantime the groom first visited Talla's house with his uncle to ask for her hand, and then they returned to hear her father's reply. On the day they were married, they both sat on the ground, Talla on one side of her father and Sardar on the other, heads lowered, eyes downcast. The mullah recited the marriage ceremony and asked for their consent. They said "yes" and the mullah pronounced them man and wife.

The day Sardar left, Talla's family came down from the upper village and joined all of the lower village as they gathered around him to pray and say their farewells. Talla was allowed to stand at the front. When the time came for him to begin his journey, Sardar spoke to his wife for the first time with a simple goodbye.

"May God keep you," she replied.

For three years Talla waited for her husband. It was known that he was still alive and would come for his wife. He regularly sent word with travelers who stopped in Kashan and passed on his news to a tradesman who, in turn, transmitted it to a Ghamsari. The news was always brief: Sardar was well, he was working hard to set himself up, and would soon come for his wife. No one doubted his honest intentions; he was a good man, a worker, a man of faith. No one thought for a moment he might take another woman and not come for his wife. No one, except Talla.

Here as in other places, girls were prepared for marriage from the earliest age. They were often told, "When you're married you'll need to know how to do such-and-such, a married woman does so-and-so . . . " Nine is the age for marriage. Some are betrothed earlier, usually to a cousin; others are told one fine day who is to be their husband for life and all eternity.

Talla's friends and cousins the same age as her were almost all already married. Those who were not did not number among the loveliest, nor the strongest. A widower or a man with little wealth, with few of life's blessings, would marry one or another of them someday.

Talla was married, though, and she longed to celebrate her marriage and wear the jewel her husband would give her. She wanted her own home and children.

But the truth was—contrary to her ardent wish to be a woman, to be indoors running her own household—Talla was still a child who flourished out of doors. What she loved most in the world was working in the open air, in the fields and orchards. She was unhappy when her mother asked her to sweep a room or wash the linen. Not that she was lazy—far from it. She was always willing to work. However hard the task, even in the cold and snow, she was not discouraged. Only, she needed fresh air and space. When she was surrounded by nature, looking at the mountains, talking to God and the Prophet, handling roses, touching water and soil, she remembered the stories people told of fairies and giants, and was happy.

When she stood motionless by the washhouse, though, Talla was dejected, sometimes even anguished. The anxiety that gnawed at her was not fear that Sardar might die or be taken away by an earthquake, an epidemic, or a flood. No, it was something else: another woman coming into her husband's life . . . and the thought of it was killing her. She spoke of this to holy Fatima and asked for her blessing. "It would kill me," she told her. Sardar was her man, her man who had had the courage to leave, to go see the world, to live in the capital. She was the wife of this strong man, and no one should take him from her. But she was so weak and he so far away! Her only consolation was in prayer. So she suggested an agreement with God: She would address one hundred salvations to him every day and in exchange God would watch over her husband for her. She believed in God and his promises. But she also had to beware black magic and the spells women could cast. So when she was wracked with anxiety she would address still more salvations to God to ward off all evil. "God is great, he will protect you," her aunt Gohar told her.

The first winter after Sardar left, Talla told herself she must wait till the spring, because winter is not a good time to travel. Then she persuaded herself Sardar would be back at the end of spring, for the Festival of the Rose, when the fragrance from

Mohamed's flowers fills the air with enchantment for miles around Ghamsar, when people sing traditional songs, ask for God's blessing, sacrifice lambs, and heat great vats side by side, some for the roses, others for the lambs.

S pring came and went, without Sardar. The following
winter was cold and harsh, like Talla's life.

Talla's house had an upper floor. The main room on the
ground floor was the heart of family life. A host of little
recesses carved into the earth walls housed bowls, placemats,
lamps . . . At the far end, mattresses and blankets were stacked
neatly into two piles as tall as a man. In winter they set up the
korsi, a low table covered with a huge blanket under which
they kept a heating pan filled with glowing embers and hot
stones. The family would come together and sleep huddled
around the *korsi*. In the morning the cock's crow served to
wake them, and each member of the family immediately knew
what his or her duty was: one went to fetch water, another lit
the lamp, a third made the tea. They breakfasted around the
korsi in the warmth of the last embers, under the thick blanket
that still harbored some of the night's heat. Then, from the
youngest to the eldest, they each set about their day's tasks.

The room opened out onto a terrace with three steps leading down to the yard. An exterior staircase led to the upstairs
room where the family stored all their wealth: their linen,
crockery, and tools, as well as provisions and harvests. In winter, bags of dried fruit and salted meat preserved in fat were
hung from the ceiling. In summer, the parents slept in this
room, away from the children. A long ladder gave access to the
flat roof of the house where large trays of fruit, vegetables, and
herbs were laid out to dry every day in the hot season.

The hens, the donkey, and a few sheep lived together in the yard. A well, a basin, and the oven dug into the bare earth fulfilled every domestic need. Beyond lay an extensive garden where all sorts of different fruit trees grew side by side. Talla's father also owned a parcel of land a little farther south, at the foot of the mountain where the Persian roses grew. Complicated earthworks channeled water from the river to a faraway village but also to Ghamsar's various neighborhoods and gardens. No one was short of water, and the plantations flourished.

Talla's family was large, with five children: two girls and three boys. Her younger sister, Havva, was four that year. A good, gentle child, she, too, had green eyes, and she never left Talla's side. From the moment she was born, Talla had taken responsibility for her. In such families, it was often the older girls' role to look after the little ones in order to help their parents and learn their future job as mothers.

When Havva was six months old and Talla only six, she had carried her on her back, fed her, wiped her nose, and sung her lullabies. Later they enjoyed running through the valley together. Talla dreamed of having Havva in Tehran with her, she would like to find a husband for her there and send for her.

But Havva had a failing that angered her parents: at the age of four she was still wetting her bed at night. The soiled mattress and blanket had to be washed every time. That winter her father beat her with a stick on several occasions to teach her to grow up, but still she could not.

The two girls went for walks through the thick snow, and when Talla pulled the collar of her sister's jacket around her neck to protect it from the cold or arranged her scarf to keep her ears nice and warm, she would often talk about this issue. She told Havva she must stop doing it at night, especially in winter, because then they all slept around the *korsi*, and when she wet her bed their mother had to wash the big blanket,

which took a long time to dry. In the meantime they had to
cover the *korsi* with lots of little blankets that slipped and fell
off. This let the heat out, and their father would get cold in the
night, then in the morning, irritable after a bad night's sleep, he
would beat her all the harder. Like the last time when she was
beaten twice for the same nocturnal incident. Havva cried and
her tears rolled over cheeks red with cold. Her green eyes went
red, too, growing still more beautiful. And she said she didn't
do it on purpose, it happened in the night when she was
asleep, that someone or something must want to hurt her,
maybe the devil had got inside her. To ward off this idea Talla
asked her sister to bite her tongue and stop her nonsense, then
Talla bit the flesh of her own hand between her thumb and
index finger, then turned the hand over and bit it again, and
recited a verse from the Koran. Talla thought they should go
see the mullah, he would know what to do. But her father
would never agree to that, it was shameful to take your daughter to the mullah because she was wetting the bed aged four.
So they would have to go see Mehr, the healer in the lower village who wrote charms and prepared potions. Her parents
would not like that either: you had to pay for the woman's
services. "We're really not going to pay for this stupid urine
business!" they would say. Her aunt Gohar said Havva had to
drink an infusion of yellow dead-nettle to strengthen her blad-
der. But their mother had so many children she had no time to
make infusions for Havva. Talla would willingly have done it,
only where could she find dead-nettles in winter? Her father
could have given her money to buy them from the herbalist,
Mirza Amir, but he would never do that. How sad!

It was an icy morning when all of Ghamsar was blanketed in snow. In the half light of their mud house the smell of yesterday's cooking mingled with the sweat of men who stopped washing through the winter, the stench of the animals they tended, and the waft of the embers in the *korsi*. When Havva woke to the cock's crow and realized her bed was wet again, her eyes filled with tears and her mouth started to quiver. Terrified, she looked over to her father. With just one glance, he understood and his face hardened immediately. It was as if it was a father's duty to be merciless at the sight of his children's fear: Instead of softening him, Havva's terror sharpened his anger.

"I'm going to teach you a lesson you won't forget!" he bellowed. And he instructed his wife to remove Havva's underwear. Her mother made no protest. The thought of having to clean the big blanket that lay over the *korsi* yet again had made her angry too. Havva's father took the fire tongs and looked inside the brazier for a glowing log that had stayed alight all night. He found one and told Havva to spread her legs. Havva opened them wide, offered no resistance. Held in the tongs, the log cast the last of its light in the shadowy dawn. No one had thought to light the lamp yet. The ember came closer to Havva, and Talla, whose eyes were wide with horror, started to shake. There was no escape from this abomination, and she knew it. But Havva could not believe it would happen, she watched the scorching ember come closer and could not believe it: it wasn't possible, he wouldn't do it, someone would stop him, himself, her mother, someone else, or something out of the sky. In horrified silence the family stood petrified, watching the ember's glowing trajectory through the darkness. The father brought it down between Havva's legs and held it there a moment. He actually did it.

A scream of pain and disbelief tore through the half light and hit them full in the face before reverberating around the entire village. Then the wind picked up this child's wail and carried it off into the mountains. And Talla thinks she can still hear that agonized scream resonating as she leaves the village along Mount Ashke.

But before that, while the ember sizzled against Havva's delicate skin, Talla shrieked: "*Ya ghamar-e bani hashem!*"

Havva did not have time to forget the lesson she had been taught by her father. She died within a week. She died in appalling pain, with this burn between her legs, peering with her own green eyes into the green eyes of her sister Talla who sat beside her. Weeping, one for the other's pain, the other in shame. Each a mirror of her sister, without words, both innocent.

No one but Talla wept for Havva. Children are born in great numbers here and die for nothing. Besides, this child was not in good health, there was something not right about her, she would have gone soon, one way or another. Talla alone wore mourning, convinced that, had her husband been there, had she had her own home, she would have let her sister sleep at her house so she could wet her bed without shame, and the tragedy would never have happened.

When Havva was gone, Talla lay motionless in a corner for days. Until her father booted her in the back and bellowed, "Get yourself up and go help your mother." So she took herself off to the washhouse and thrust her hands into the icy water.

She carried on weeping in silence, her tears falling on the snow and pitting it with tiny crevasses just as her husband's absence lacerated her heart. He alone had some right over her, he alone would have stood up to her father, and still he was not here. So she looked up at the sky and wanted to howl with grief, but that was when she saw an eagle. And that eagle flying over her head was a sign.

Winter passed and spring came. It was Talla's turn to light the oven in the yard in the mornings. When the cock crowed she rose automatically, still half asleep, put on her shoes and cardigan, went out of the house, took some wood from the pile, lifted the small board over the oven, arranged a few logs at the back of the cavity, and lit the fire. One morning, still befuddled by sleep, she had only just put her hand on the pile of wood when a sharp pain made her scream. Her father leapt outside and saw Talla clutching her hand as if she had been burned. He took her hand and immediately recognized a snake bite on her palm. He roared at his wife to bring some belts, and wrapped one tightly around Talla's wrist, then another around her arm, all the while instructing the children to fetch pails of milk from the room on the first floor. In the meantime he sucked on the bite and spat out the venom in disgust. When he put his daughter's hand in the first pail of milk it curdled instantly. He moved to the second pail, with the same result. In the third pail, the milk remained unchanged. "She's saved!" he cried triumphantly. In his euphoria, he uncharacteristically took Talla's head in his hands and kissed her.

"If you'd died, how could I have told your husband! You can't give a man a corpse for a wife!"

The snake was never found. For several days the whole village lived in fear, people constantly looking behind them, under mattresses, within blankets. Children were frightened to go near firewood.

Talla, whom the villagers now attributed with the aura of a survivor, was peculiarly pleased by this event. It was the message from the eagle overhead: The snake had come to give her her womanhood and give her back her father. The executioner had become a savior. And, more significantly, three days after the snakebite she had her first period, and the pain that went with it, it was the price she had to pay. "A woman is revealed through pain," her aunt Gohar told her. "You'll see, every time you do your duty as a woman, there will be pain. Periods, your wedding night, childbirth . . . you might as well embrace it and cherish it. Drink it like tea which is as bitter as poison the first time, but later, if you accept it, it warms your heart."

A year later, in the autumn, at fruit-picking time, Talla was gathering walnuts at the bottom of the garden. Her back hurt from all the bending, so she stood up and stretched. That was when she saw a man silhouetted in the distance. She thought of Sardar but immediately chided herself. It couldn't be, it wasn't springtime. But as the man approached his face gradually took shape: It could be Sardar. Talla's heart started to beat so hard she pressed her hand to her chest to stop it exploding. She knew that when she faced him she would never be able to contain all the emotion and resentment she had buried inside her for three years, so she had long dreaded this meeting.

Sardar reeled for a moment. In just one glance he saw Talla's beauty, the metamorphosis that had taken place in her. He had left behind a nine-year-old, a child, now he saw her at age twelve: a woman. He looked at her openly. It was the first time he had looked her in the eye; even when they had said their farewells he had kept his eyes lowered. Now he discovered a woman's clearly defined contours, and saw in the deep green of her eyes something untamed, a suggestion of rancor, even a hint of hatred, but also perhaps something more unsettling: desire. At last he consented to say, "Hello."

By way of a reply, he received a resounding slap. The shock of it made Sardar step back. Then he mastered his emotions but did not react. He did not return the blow, did not raise his voice, ask for explanations, or try to calm her, but kept on looking her in the eye. Something neither he nor she had expected had just happened, something legitimate, something sincere, something that concerned only the two of them. Sardar now knew that his wife was a sensible man's nightmare, and he did not believe himself to be sensible; she was therefore his dream.

Slowly, ardently, their eyes communicated the inexpressible truths Sardar could not put into words: That he had thought of her every day and every night over those three years, that she had been the source of his strength, that so long as he had slept on a bed of straw with the animals he would not come for her, that, once he was working as a day laborer, he waited till he had decent lodgings and his own flock of sheep before coming for her, that it had been three years because it had taken all that time to escape poverty. Alone as a dog in the merciless rigors of a city filled with battalions of the poor, he had held out, just for her, for her honor and her pride.

Then Sardar spoke at last: "We'll play this however you prefer. Either you stay here and I send you money regularly, or I agree to a divorce, or you come with me. I'll accept your decision."

Talla replied without a moment's hesitation.

"I'm coming with you."

Talla wanted to leave straightaway. No marriage ceremony, no banquet. Just leave. There was now nothing
and no one to tie her to this place; her life was to be
elsewhere, her happiness, too. She told her husband this, right
there in the orchard. They agreed: In a week, when the donkey
was sufficiently rested, when Sardar had spent some time with
his family and the rest of the village, when he had prayed in
Soliman's mausoleum in the lower village and in the Imam
Hussein mosque, they would leave together.

Talla's father knew she still held Havva's death against him.
And he held this rancor against her. He had not meant to kill
Havva, he had meant to teach her a lesson, but that lesson had
killed her. They were the only two people who deemed him
cruel, the two people still tormented by it, his daughter and
himself. Let her go, let her go soon. Perhaps memories of
Havva would fade with those of Talla? Perhaps . . .

To express his gratitude to Talla's father for keeping and
feeding his wife for three years, Sardar gave him a string of
prayer beads from Mecca and some money wrapped in a
length of cloth. In her father's presence, Sardar gave Talla four
gold bracelets. He also sacrificed a sheep to protect them from
the evils that might befall them on their journey. They gave one
haunch to the mullah so that he might pray for them. They also
shared out a good proportion of the meat to some of the less
fortunate in the village. And with what was left they prepared
a farewell feast and invited both families and the village leader.

The evening of the very day Sardar arrived, Talla packed her belongings and joined Sardar's family. She took little with her, her clothes, her winter coat, and her wedding mirror. As she was to leave the village, the two families had reached an agreement: There would be no dowry or jointure.

That night a nuptial room was prepared for them in Sardar's home. Talla's mother talked to Talla before letting her go, explaining frankly what would happen. Sardar only just knew himself. He had had many opportunities to visit brothels in Tehran, but had made a point of refraining: it would not have pleased God or the Prophet, and mostly because a man should take his own wife and not another man's or a woman who is no one's wife. But he thought he knew, he had heard talk of this. They were shown respectfully and ceremoniously into the room where the immaculate nuptial bed awaited. They lay down side by side. Talla was calm, intimidated but content, at last her life as a woman could begin. Sardar was far more frightened than Talla. She was surprised: he hurt her. So it really was true that a woman is revealed with pain. She bled, honor was preserved. They left the bloodstained sheet—someone would come to check it—and emerged from the room to join the cheering well-wishers, who had waited outside. Sardar's mother was no longer alive so it was his older brother's wife who went to check; and she reappeared intoning the song of a consummated marriage.

Talla displayed the beauty, pride, and restraint of girls whose virginity has been taken legitimately. A distinctive grace that appears only once on a woman's face. Every man who laid eyes on her at that moment was gripped with searing desire, and the women with equally fierce jealousy. Sardar stood with his head lowered and a smile on his lips. He too had just had an initiation, into the carnal world of manhood.

The following day Talla was taken to the hammam. A celebration for women alone. They sang frivolous songs and

laughed out loud. They danced naked and talked of their experiences as wives. The youngest among them dreamed of the
future, the oldest wept for the past, saying they were shedding
"tears of joy offered to the young bride."

Sardar went to the hammam, too. Men are more discreet
with each other: They congratulated him and honored him, but
did not dwell on the subject. On the other hand, they all desperately wanted to hear of his adventures in Tehran. Sardar was
not a naturally talkative man, but was particularly quiet that
day. He now felt different from them, he believed he was a
townsman. He told them the city was big and there were lots of
people but that the sky was the same color wherever you were.
What more could he tell them, and what would be the point?
What could they understand? He told them he had livestock
and tended them himself. Without resorting to exaggeration—
he was afraid of lying, it would not please God—he led them to
understand that he had done well, that he was richer there than
he had been in Ghamsar. He raised his voice slightly so that his
uncle could hear him clearly, and his uncle heard. It was the
most glorious moment of Sardar's life.

The rest, the thousand other things he longed to describe,
he kept for Talla. The journey to Tehran was long, and he
intended to while it away with his stories.

In very few words he said enough that morning for the
gathering of naked men in the steam of the hammam to envy
him and curse him. For legends sprang from the insolence of
men who achieved too much and could not disguise their
pride. These men who returned to the village, gripped by a
contained suffering that went by the name of exile, fascinated
but also repelled the villagers, like the pride and fear of a man
who has a tiger at his feet or the love of a woman too beautiful
for him. Because these men forced every one of their listeners
to make a bitter appraisal of himself, of his cautiousness and
cowardice in living a life devoid of daring or regret.

S ardar was now recognized as the new village brave and five days later he stood before his clan with his head held high as he loaded the donkey with enough dried fruit, cheese, dried meat, and water to last ten days. Then he helped Talla onto her mount. The mullah held the Koran aloft for them to walk beneath it, and gave Talla a stone from Ghamsar, telling her to leave it by the side of the road when she saw the dome of Saint Fatima's mausoleum. Another stone added to all those accumulated over time by pilgrims who had gone before her and had laid eyes on the dome of that sacred mausoleum for the first time. The mullah told her that when she left this stone she was to make a wish, and he asked her to pray for the village. As he said these words, the mullah had tears in his eyes, for he, too, believed that outsiders who came to Ghamsar left behind their evil eye. He did everything he could to ward off these curses, but ill fate reigned supreme, and so he wept. The mullah was a simple man with a strong sense of duty. He might well have accepted the haunch he was offered when a sheep was sacrificed, but he never failed to make the promised prayer in return. He was a man who believed in God, the Prophet, and every word he himself spoke about religion. And so he wept. In Iran men weep as readily as women.

The whole village was there. They prayed, they clasped the young couple to their hearts, then the donkey set off. Talla turned around one last time to see the villagers gathered behind her, and thought this more beautiful than a marriage ceremony. Few women had left like this before her. An aunt of hers, they said, a woman with blue eyes, but Talla had not known her, she had left before she was born. Talla would be remembered far more readily than if she had stayed in the village. People would say: "My sister, my aunt, my neighbor, Talla, the one who went to Tehran . . . "

Perched on the donkey, Talla follows the path that runs along Mount Ashke, to the north of Ghamsar, and thinks she hears Havva's scream of pain one last time. Her tears fall. She weeps for the whole village, for her family and friends, for Mohamed's flower, for Imamzadeh, and for Havva. But also because she is afraid. Afraid to go beyond the mountain. What if there really are monsters on the other side? What if, once she has left her paradise, she finds hell as it has been described to her: People burning in fires while boiling oil is poured down their throats and their sides are pierced with lances, and this for all eternity?

What lies beyond the mountains? She knows the word desert, but what does it really mean? In Tehran, the royal entourage is passionate about photographs, but of course Talla has never seen one, still less one of the desert. Talla has lived for twelve years in a star-shaped green valley between mountains that change color with the passing seasons: purplish gray in summer, brown in the fall, and white in winter and spring. She sometimes thought she could see djinns, and one time she even met a jackal on the path. She knows the secrets of rosewater. She knows about death and snakebites, and now even love. But she knows nothing beyond these mountains.

Talla and Sardar will come down from the mountains and cross the desert to reach Kashan, then they will head north, covering 150 miles to reach Tehran, the country's capital. It is the year 1299 in the Iranian calendar: the end of a century and the imminent end of a dynasty. For now Talla is still in the mountains of western Iran and does not know the king's name. She has never heard the words history, geography, Asia, Europe, Russia, or England. She has never heard about Iran's constitutional revolution in 1285, nor the Bolshevik revolution in Russia, and does not know that the First World War has only just come to an end. She does not know that Sardar was born the year William Knox D'Arcy secured the concession for Iranian oil before even finding a single drop of it; that she herself was born the year oil was struck at Masjed Soleyman, and that her birth coincided with that of the Anglo-Persian Oil Company. She has never heard of Sattar Khan, Baqer Khan, Yeprem Khan, Mirza Kouchek Khan, Khiabani . . . Iran's heroes and martyrs of the last few years. Just as she does not even realize a town called Tabriz exists, and knows even less about the social democrats or Bandar-e Anzali and his communists.

Neither has she ever heard of the "Farangs" who live in far-away western territories; she does not know that in the capital she will meet the men, women, customs, and languages of the Turks, Kurds, Turkmen, Qashqai, Arabs, Bakhtiari, Fars, Lurs, Gilaki, Mazanderani, and Baloch who live in Iran's own feudal territories.

What lies beyond the mountains?

II
GOHAR,
THE CHILD MOTHER'S ANGEL

After ten days of traveling, Talla arrives in Sharh-e Rey, completely veiled. In Ghamsar, women wore the chador only for prayers and religious ceremonies, and they wore white ones or colorful ones. Granted, in day to day life they wore long scarves knotted behind their heads, but their hair was not entirely covered and they made no particular effort to hide the braids that hung down their backs.

Sardar had brought a black chador and a white *roubandeh* from Tehran. As soon as they were beyond the mountain he asked Talla to wear them. He asked gently. Sardar is not authoritarian, he enjoys securing another person's consent to what he believes is just or necessary. He explained that in towns and cities women wore the chador to hide themselves from men's eyes, it was required by religion there. Talla accepted without protest, slightly amused, even enthusiastic. She thought that by wearing the new garment she would become a part of this other world. So she accepted the costume of what she saw as a game: she put on the black chador and attached the white *roubandeh* across her forehead, letting it cover her whole face and neck.

So Talla is dressed in black as she arrives in Shahr-e Rey, a small town a few miles south of Tehran. Sardar has made his home here with no idea of its history. No one remembers its glory days or the stages of its decline, apart from the Mongol invasion which has never been erased from Iranian collective memory. To this day they say that an untidy house has been invaded by the Mongols.

The town Talla comes to was built not far from the ruins of the fallen city. As the religious center of Zoroastrianism and standing as it did on the silk road, it survived from one era to the next. Sacked by Alexander then destroyed by an earthquake, it was rebuilt by the Persian kings, who relit the town's sacred fire. After the arrival of Islam, it briefly became the country's capital and was the apogee of art and culture, competing with Baghdad itself. Then it was irretrievably ravaged by the Mongols and reduced to ashes by Timur.

Not far from Shahr-e Rey, which has become a suburb of its own former suburb Tehran, Sardar has found lodgings in the fortified village of Hadji Agha Ahmad, and has settled his sheep here.

The first thing Talla is astonished to discover is a new social order: master and peasants. Here, the village belongs to the master and the peasants bow to their master. In this country of feudal lords, Ghamsar never belonged to anyone, was not part of any estate or tribe and was not ruled by any khan. In Ghamsar each individual owned his own house and land, some were richer, others not so rich, and there were a few who were unclassifiable and were called idiots or described as disturbed. And of course there was the village chief, who was chosen by the heads of families. He was owed respect and consideration but no one bowed before him. He was addressed courteously but men like Talla's father spoke to him as equals. Naturally he gave orders to the young—fetch this for me, do that for me—and when something needed straightening out, a conflict to resolve or separating people who were beating each other with sticks over some water or a disputed plot of land, he could raise his voice and establish his authority. It goes without saying, it was better to have him on one's side, but no one bowed before him. There was also the mullah, who was highly regarded, but that was to do with God and the Prophet. Here in Rey, the peasants are afraid of the master. Here, even if you work hard, the master can drive you out overnight without any explanation if it suits him. The master is absolute lord of his land. Luckily Sardar rents only one room from him, and has his own sheep.

In this master, Talla finds someone more powerful and terrifying than her father. When she left Ghamsar, she believed that no one but God and her husband would have authority over her. This pleasure is swiftly spoiled, and the solid ground of her ancestors has given way to shifting sands. "Damn the desert," she thinks.

Talla now turns to Sardar to discuss this. With her husband away for three years, she had all the time she needed to imagine him as she pleased. In fact, once Havva was dead she lived only for him and with him. She devoted herself—her untouched self—to him; she dedicated her every move and word to him. At every moment he was there with her, exactly as she would wish him to be. Then Sardar arrived and they spent five days together in Ghamsar, five days and five nights to get to know each other, to discover and savor their naked bodies, a man's and a woman's, and the love that arose from them. Next came the journey and its surprises. And Sardar has not faltered. He has remained steadfast, a man who confronts every situation, by her side and respectful of her. So it is only natural for her to turn to him. He is her man, he will be able to answer her questions. Sardar keeps patiently telling her, as often as need be, that the aim is to work hard for a few years so they can buy their own house; then they will be masters in their own home. In the end she agrees that Sardar's plan is acceptable, particularly as hard work is nothing new to her. For Talla, work is the most natural and most sacred thing in life. Like a fetish, work protects her; like a sponge, it absorbs her doubts, anesthetizes her. And so she throws herself into it. It is the only solution, the only way to escape the latent fear that holds Rey in its sly grip. She can feel the fear in everyone. Fear of the master, but not only that, fear of something more important than him, of the king and his court. In Ghamsar, the king was viewed as a distant power, one that was itself subjected to the omnipotence of God. God and then the king, necessities to establish a stable, orderly world. Both invisible, both real. In Rey the master is like the king, and the actual king is close by in Tehran. In Rey there is talk of the king, his name is spoken, things are known about him. He could even come here in person. Here, a peasant must bow his head and not look powerful men in the eye, he must know how to be invisible. Because each of them, from the master right up to the king—via their representatives—has rights over him, while he has rights over no one.

Now twelve, after three years of waiting and impatience, Talla has left behind her paradise to come to the land of men. She has worn the chador and *roubandeh* since leaving the mountain, and for the last few days of their journey she found them more bothersome than anything, but they are now a protection from the perils of the world. She is inside, they are outside. Under her chador, she can feel fear, anger, or sadness, but no one will ever know. No man can lift her *roubandeh* and see her frightened eyes. She can even glare at him furiously, and he would be none the wiser. Now there, God is more powerful than the king, she thinks. So she decides never to lift her *roubandeh*. Even though peasant women are not strictly bound by custom and, when working, usually remove their *roubandeh* and wear their chadors tied at the waist, Talla does not raise hers in public.

And Sardar gradually comes to like this exclusivity. The fact that Talla's gleaming green eyes, whose passionate directness fills him with scalding desire, are kept for him alone, the fact that her long thick hair, delicate neck, and fine mouth are revealed to him alone proves so irresistibly voluptuous that he finds he wants her to be veiled from head to toe so that he can constantly succumb to the delicious pleasure of completely unveiling her all for himself alone.

S o Talla puts her trust in God and her husband, and settles into her new home: one of the rooms that forms a circle around the master's courtyard. Sardar has everything ready, the bedding, the tableware, and a lamp. It all seems adequately comfortable to Talla. She lights the lamp, puts the mirror she has brought from Ghamsar onto the shelves on a wall, stows her bundle of clothes in an alcove, and sets to work, doing what she does best, making butter, cream, yogurt, and cheese. This is what she wanted—her own home with her husband by her side—and with a happy heart, she prepares for a peaceful life. But in the depths of winter news reaches them: There has been a coup. The Cossack brigade that guards the royal family has occupied Tehran under their leader Reza Khan. This Cossack brigade is one of the ideas that Naser al-Din Shah brought back from his travels abroad. On this occasion he was impressed by the military parade organized in his honor in Russia, and asked the tsar to lend him some Russian officers to set up a new military force in Iran. It is these same officers who, under Reza Khan's command, occupied Tehran on E*sfand* 3rd, 1299.

Abdollah, the master's handyman, spreads the news. The peasants panic and wonder, "And what does the master say?"

"I heard him say that Ahmad Shah is not even twenty-five! That since he came to the throne at the age of twelve he's just been a puppet king, with no army and no wealth. He says it's the English who really have the power in court, that they're sitting on the oil fields in the south and lending the country's money to the king while they ask for one concession after another. Meanwhile on the other side, the Russians with their Bolshevism are helping the revolutionaries in the north who are working toward an Iranian socialist republic! And he says it's actually the local feudal lords who rule throughout Iran. It's hardly surprising he was toppled by his own royal guard!"

"Allahu Akbar!"

All that day the peasants and shepherds peer anxiously into the distance, standing in the cold waiting for soldiers to arrive. Sardar asks Talla to gather together her things and prepare some food in case they have to leave in a hurry. "To go where?" Talla asks. "There are no mountains here! The mountains are over there!"—and she points toward the north—"They're easy enough to see, but they're so far away. Even if we ran, it would take us two days to reach them." In Ghamsar they always knew that if there was an invasion or an attack they would have to run away across the mountain, first the women and children, then, if need be, the men. The mountains were the Ghamsari's advantage over the enemy; they knew them like the back of their hands. Talla herself once set off into the mountain with Havva on her back. Someone had screamed, "Looters! Run, run!" Talla was picking fruit in the orchard and understood the instruction; she dropped everything, took Havva on her back, and ran toward the mountains. They spent the night there with other villagers, sleeping on the bare earth, and someone came to fetch them the next day.

"We'll go wherever the others go," Sardar tells her.

Luckily, no troops came; no shots, no thunder of cannon, no war. So it was nothing to do with them. Talla unpacked her bundle and Sardar went back to his jobs. And Ahmad Shah immediately appointed Reza Khan as commander in chief of the army.

A period of long peregrinations began now for Talla as she followed the transhumance every year. In winter the shepherds kept their flocks at Shahr-e Rey, and in summer they took them north to Shemiran, at the foot of the Alborz mountains. They never went into Tehran, though, always skirting around it.

In three years Sardar had been to Tehran only once. When he first left Ghamsar he had stopped in Shahr-e Rey, believing he had reached Tehran. And yet, unlike other immigrants, he spoke the same language as the local inhabitants: Persian. But he had no real desire to mix with people or communicate with them. Sardar had always liked keeping his distance, living in silence, contemplating the world from above like a solitary eagle. He needed his horizon to be clear so he could see only the essence of life, as it was at the outset, before words existed; having people around, their chatter and bustle, interrupted the view.

By the time Sardar realized Tehran was a little farther on, he had already found work in Shahr-e Rey so he stayed there. The urge to visit the capital gnawed away at him, though. As he was not a frivolous man, he waited until he had a good reason to visit: His return to Ghamsar three years later provided that opportunity. He surely couldn't go back to his village without seeing the capital. When he left, he had said, "I'm going to Tehran." And so he decided to go there to buy his wedding gifts.

He headed straight for the bazaar and strolled through its narrow alleys and the various quarters devoted to particular crafts: the carpet bazaar, the goldsmiths' bazaar, the spice bazaar, and so on. Marveling at such abundance, at this profusion of goods, he stopped in one of the bazaar's cafés and he, who was usually so unforthcoming, had actually joined in conversation with the men drinking tea around him.

"Allahu Akbar! Where does so much splendor come from?"

"Aha, everything you see here is nothing compared to what you cannot see: the all-encompassing power of the stallholders!" one of the men said.

"They're the most influential men in the country. When times are hard, the thing the king dreads most is the *bazaaris* striking," another whispered in his ear. "The day the *bazaaris* closed their shutters and the alleys of the bazaar were filled with a deathly hush, the king up there in his palace heard the silence of his own death."

"Oh, the *bazaaris*! They've controlled everything for the last few years, and it's not over yet . . . "

Sardar felt that what he had seen and heard in Tehran was shameless, disturbing, and far beyond his grasp. "A man must know his place" became his new motto. He came to the conclusion that "Tehran is not for us," and for years he avoided the city. But Tehran never failed to intrigue Talla when she saw it in the distance as she traveled from Shahr-e Rey to Shemiran in late spring, and on her return trip in the fall.

When the time came for the shepherds to move their flocks to new pastures, their families went with them. For five years Talla spent the three summer months with Sardar in Shemiran, to the north of Tehran, in the foothills of Damavand, Iran's highest peak. She enjoyed their time here; it reminded her of Ghamsar with its cool air, bright water, and flower-filled gardens.

The first summer was pure enchantment. She walked the hills of Shemiran with Sardar, herding the sheep, gazing at the mountains, and sleeping under the stars. And it was on one of those hillsides in the shade of an old plane tree and beneath the placid eye of their sheep that they conceived their first child one summer's afternoon.

Talla returned to Rey three months pregnant and full of life and hope.

But as soon as she was back in the village fortified by Hadji Agha Ahmad, she was confronted with the locals' macabre gossip. All that the peasants could talk about was the socialist republic in the Gilan region and Mirza Kouchek Khan's severed head. He was the symbolic leader of the Jangali rebels from the northern forest.

The hawker who came to sell salt in the village had met a fellow from Rasht in Tehran: "He saw Mirza Kochek Khan's severed head with his own eyes; it was being paraded around the square by soldiers. By all accounts, his head was then sent to Reza Khan, who had it buried without the body, and one of the dead man's followers dug it up in the night to take it back to Rasht."

"And what does the master say?" everyone asked Abdullah.

"The master couldn't care less! All he is interested in are Reza Khan's maneuverings with the four parties. Because there are four, you know: conservatives in the reformist party, reformists in the Modernity party, socialists, and even communists," Abdullah said, counting them out on his fingers. "He says Reza Khan wants to have his laws voted in by parliament without attracting the fury of the mullahs, so he makes alliances with one group to pass a particular law, and then with others for different laws."

"They say he had blue eyes," the hawker said.

"Who? Reza Khan?"

"No, Mirza Kouchek Khan."

"That's interesting! Everyone knows you have to beware of people with blue eyes, you never know where they're from . . . "

Then, whether he had heard them or simply made them up, the hawker reported the horrors Mirza had committed, and those that were inflicted on him.

The rest of it was of little interest to the locals. As were Reza Khan's dubious arrangements with parliament. They knew nothing of the arcane rites and titles of the one thousand powerful families that mattered in the country; their intrigues and pacts, which were the favorite tidbits of Tehran's bourgeois society, meant nothing here. Unfortunately.

Talla tells Sardar that this tittle-tattle about Mirza Kouchek Khan's hideous death is a bad omen; Sardar nods his head but says nothing. In the image Talla constructed of him while she waited for him in Ghamsar, he talked more. But the real Sardar talks little, he is all caresses, eye contact, and smiles. And Talla speaks for two, because everything is necessary to make up a life, and nothing can replace anything else. And a misunderstood silence is more brutal that the most spiteful words, the void it creates more empty than any unspeaking mouth.

And while Reza Khan's expedient alliances progress, Talla's pregnancy does not. Age thirteen and six months pregnant, she gives birth to a stillborn baby girl with long black hair. She most likely loses her because she has not been careful enough. She has been lifting heavy loads and carrying water, milk, lambs . . . and out on the plains, when she was alone with Sardar, she would take off her chador and blithely run in every direction and climb trees. But her young body could not be both a mother and a child. It was a difficult labor and she was devastated when she saw her stillborn child. She wept for a long time. She held the little creature in her arms for a couple of hours, called her Gohar, after her beloved aunt, and sang lullabies to her, as she used to in Ghamsar. She had once found a lifeless bird whose body was still warm, and she had held it in her hand and stroked it for several minutes, and all at once the bird had beat its wings and taken flight. Alas, she could not bring her daughter back to life.

For the rest of her life she would talk tenderly to Gohar because she was as beautiful as an angel, and had long dark hair.

Talla gradually recovered from her grief and life resumed, set to the rhythm of the flock's movements. Only, she did not conceive again quickly. After a year, she started to worry. Prayer was the first recourse. She asked God's forgiveness every day for sins she had committed without realizing it— although sometimes she did realize, such as when she spoke ill of someone or other. But another year went by with no result and so she sought other remedies. She consulted an herbalist who made her a preparation of herbs to improve her fertility. To no avail. Then she saw an amulet-maker to have her own talisman. To no effect.

Only the army's movements distracted Talla from her

burdensome lot as a woman. This army was ever larger, ever better equipped, and she felt she could see it approach from far, far away, through the noise and dust, as soldiers came and went, quashing uprisings in every corner of Iran.

The rest of the time she was obsessed by her own reputation. A woman who bears no children is an anomaly. In the fertile breeding pond of their fortified village, well-meaning neighbors wanted to see her pregnant at all costs. So they offered—no, insisted she take—their remedies. Older women stood in for the mother Talla did not have by her side, asking her intrusive questions about her private life, about Sardar's vigor. They came knocking at her door: "My girl, you must let him fertilize you once on the night before the full moon and then again on the night after the full moon. There will be a full moon tomorrow so it must be this evening, and when his water is in you, you must not move from your bed, you must hold your legs together and pray that it will take." And they waited for a report the next morning: "So, is it done? Tell me you didn't move afterward? Don't forget you need to do it again tomorrow evening . . . "

The less well-meaning were convinced she was infertile, and believed there was nothing more to hope from her: "My friend," they told Sardar, "a man should not feed a woman who will never bear a child. You need to get rid of her, replace her as soon as you can. Send her back to your village and we'll find a pretty young girl to give you sons." But Sardar was not in the least worried: a child would come when it was God's will. "I have only one wife and I shall have no other, ever. Even if she dies, I will not replace her." He said it steadily, without raising his voice, stating it as people state the truth.

At last, after two and a half years, God forgave her—at least, that was how she saw it—and she conceived again. This time she was careful all through her pregnancy, and her sixteen-year-old woman's body agreed to carry the child, and

God gave her a son. He brought great joy. A happy Sardar sacrificed a sheep in front of his son to protect him from evil. Half of the meat was distributed to the poor, because there are always those who are poorer than you. And with the other half, they made a rich stew for the rest of the village; even the master had a share, preoccupied though he was with all the new laws Reza Shah was having voted in by parliament.

Alas, this child also died. One day, when he was only six months old, Talla offered him a tiny mouthful of her own food, lamb stew with chickpeas. He liked it and craned his head for more; she gave it to him gladly; he wanted more again and she kept spoiling him till he died of indigestion. Of course when the child's eyes started rolling, Talla called for help, she ran out without her chador and screamed, neighbors came running, lots of them, pell-mell, clustering around the child who had stopped breathing and Talla who was still explaining and praying . . . when they finally told her there was no hope she screamed: "*Ya ghamar-e bani hashem!*"

Sardar was far away on the plain with his flock, a boy ran to let him know but could not find him. When Sardar finally came home that evening he saw people gathered outside his door. He needed no explanations; there was nothing to celebrate so it must be this. He smacked his head with both hands, sat down on the ground and beat his head again. Talla had been almost unconscious since the afternoon. The child was left in a corner till the next day. In the morning Sardar took him in his arms and buried him at the foot of a tree on the plain. He paid a mullah to pray for him.

Talla's grief was unbounded. The saying that bad luck comes in threes seemed to be made for her. Havva, her daughter, and now her son. The three had passed over so quickly, as if they were a burden on the world.

Sardar did not blame her for what happened, Talla would not have borne it, she wept enough as it was. "That's three now," he told her. "It will be all right now, it's over, you'll see, next time there'll be no heartbreak." But other people did blame her; everyone seemed to hold it against her. No one came to comfort her, no women from the village wanted to hold her hand in theirs and weep with her. Talla could not recover from losing her son or from the severity of their judgment. "God gives and God takes away," Sardar told her. Talla nodded but could not accept this, and she wept. "God gives and God takes away," Sardar told everyone who spoke ill of Talla. They nodded, but did not change their views. They had judged her.

Luckily, shortly after this, Abdullah announced the accession of the Pahlavi dynasty. This kept all those judgmental minds in the village busy, interrupting the snide comments about Talla for a time.

"Reza Khan has become Reza Shah. He is now king."

"What does the master say?"

"He says it's better like this. Let him be king! He says it's better for him to be king than to set up his beloved republic. God be praised, the *uluma* didn't accept it, they wouldn't have that sort of nonsense in our country."

Without truly grasping the significance of the event, Talla was relieved. But why all the fuss? What would it change? One king was replacing another without a war or a battle: From a humble peasant's home, the view was still the same. For now. But from that moment on Reza Shah started flouting Iranian tradition, and the changes would prove devastating.

The fuss was short-lived. For the peasants in Shahr-e Rey, who had to lower their heads and look at the ground in the master's courtyard, the only thing that mattered was whether the king's army would come pillaging and massacring in their homes. Reassured, they went back to their work and, at the same time, to the question of Talla's womb.

But Sardar was not prepared to let them. Toward the end of

spring, when they were preparing to make their annual journey to Shemiran, Sardar decided, "Enough is enough!" He suddenly made up his mind: He went to see the master and told him he was leaving his lodgings. Then he went to find Talla and said, "Pack everything, we won't be coming back here. They say there's lots of snow in Shemiran in winter. You tell me that at night you dream of the thick snow you knew as a child, well then, let's go!"

At eighteen, Talla sets off to make her home in Shemiran forever. Beneath her black chador, sheltered from men's prying eyes, she is a lone woman traveling. She leaves with a few bundles on the ass's back, the flock of sheep ahead of her, and her husband walking in silence, but no child. As usual, the winds of life carry her as she leaves one place for another, heavy with memories of a death. She follows the road, such is her sorrow.

Far from their families and with no friends, they mean nothing to anyone. It is just the two of them, and they will have to make do with this nothingness.

Sardar is still as silent, Talla still as talkative. That is how they balance their world, between the laconic confidence of a man who has faith in life and the chattering mistrust of a woman who expects a new misfortune to appear every day. That first night in Shemiran, then, as they prepare to sleep among their sheep out under the stars at the top of a hill, Talla loosens her black hair; it falls around her face and her shining eyes as she offers her delicate breasts to Sardar. But before she allows their bodies to seal their union once more with passion, she makes him promise that they will have their very own home here, in Shemiran.

S tretching out in the middle of Shemiran is the vast Davoudieh plain, given that name because the summer garden of Mirza Davoud Khan, son of Mirza Agha Khan Nouri, the second chancellor to Naser al-Din Shah, once flourished here. In the center of Davoudieh is a fortified Armenian village with its beautiful garden, its ice pit, and its large swimming pond. The local master is a Jew, and his house is in the middle of the village, surrounded by lodgings that he lets to peasant families, all of them Armenian. The neighboring land owned by him is marked out by centennial plane trees that bear witness to a long history, as does the abandoned hammam whose dilapidated walls are still adorned with ancient ceramic tiles.

The master lets out his land to Armenian tenant farmers who grow watermelon, wheat, and barley. He agrees to let a room and a plot of land to Sardar and Talla. Sardar keeps his flock of sheep and, to hold the promise he made to Talla, he, too, starts growing watermelon in the spring. To support her husband, Talla continues milking the ewes and making dairy products; as well as this, she puts the old village oven back to use, baking bread and sweet biscuits that she sells to the Armenians and inhabitants of the surrounding area.

Shemiran rekindles Talla's strength and hope. She feels soothed. The climate suits her better, she will at last be able to tread deep snow again, and feel the mountain so close by that it seems she could touch it simply by raising her hand. And more importantly, no one in Davoudieh seems interested in her problems with motherhood. What is more, thanks be to God, there is no fear here. The master here is clement. The peasants here are not his subjects but his tenants. And the people here are not afraid of vagrants or child snatchers or any sort of wrongdoer. Not like Tehran, where bandits, addicts, and thieves throng the streets in the neighborhood around the brothels, which is now called the "new town" and where Reza Shah has gathered together all the city's prostitutes. The people in Shahr-e Rey talked about it all the time. They said the brothel-keepers in these places stole young girls, imprisoned them, and forced them into prostitution. They were even said to steal children. Everyone was always frightened they might head a little further south to Shahr-e Rey, which was an increasingly busy stopping-off point on the way to Tehran. All sorts of people came through, people who spoke languages no one understood, who came from everywhere and nowhere. New arrivals were always viewed with suspicion.

On the other hand, the further north you go beyond Tehran, the less riffraff you see, and the better chance you have of meeting high-society folk. A great many titled and important families have summer residences in Shemiran, as do plenty of Farangi: English, Russians, and Germans, strange and distant figures who seem to have stepped out of fairy tales. These foreigners look so unreal to Talla that they seem inoffensive. Like pictures on the walls of her life. As if their existence were in another world that could not possibly coincide with hers.

S even years after the death of her first son, in a bedroom in the Armenian village and with the help of Mahtab-Khanoum, the midwife from Gholhak, Talla brought into the world a son: Bahram.

Seven years that they did not count to the rhythms of a calendar because theirs no longer existed: Reza Shah had replaced the moon with the sun. Seven years that they counted in cycles of transhumance, harvesting, and lambing . . . Seven years of longing for a child and of endless, fierce struggle with destiny.

As Talla tells it, Bahram was born when the grenadines were ripe. Which would mean his birth was in mid-fall. Only, according to his identity card, which bears the number "1," Bahram was born on the first day of the year 1312, the first day of spring. So he cannot be sure of his exact birth date. His parents probably waited a few months before registering him, time enough to be sure he would live.

"When you were born, the quinces were ready to be picked and we'd already set up the *korsi*. I remember clearly because a day or two after you were born, you were sleeping next to me under the *korsi* when All turned up and I screamed so loudly she ran away!"

"But who's All?"

"All steals newborn babies in the first four days of their lives, and swaps them for her own children or the children of djinns. Some say All was the first wife that God created for

Adam. But Adam was bound to the element earth and he fought with All, who was bound to the element fire. That's why All is so resentful, firstly of Havva but also of all women of her descent."

Sardar called his son Bahram Amir. Bahram because, in the fables told in Ghamsar, this was the name of a valiant prince and great lion hunter. In the fight for the throne after his father died, this Bahram asked that the royal crown be put between two famished lions: whoever succeeded in claiming the crown would be king. He invited his usurping adversary to try his luck first, but the challenger refused. So Bahram entered the arena, confronted the lions, killed them both, and took his crown. Bahram's legend had a profound effect on Sardar and stirred in him a passion for hunting. And Amir because it was Ghamsari and Kashani custom to use your first name followed by your father's first name. Sardar had always called himself Sardar Amir. When Reza Khan was still Prime Minister, he had introduced compulsory military service, arranged a census of the population, and instituted a system of registration: every Iranian had to be registered in order to receive an identity card clearly showing his or her family name, first name, and date and place of birth. So everyone had to choose a family name.

One day back in Shahr-e Rey, the master had summoned all the peasants to tell them that the next day government officials would come to count them and give them papers formalizing their identity. These papers would now be needed for everything they did: transactions, buying, selling, marriage, and so on. So they all needed to be in the village the following morning: men, women, and children.

The peasants had obeyed. At first light they were all there waiting for the government representatives, who were slow to arrive. The sun was already high in the sky, the flocks left untended and work left undone. The peasants grumbled and fidgeted but waited. In the middle of the afternoon, two officials arrived at last, looking exhausted. Out of respect for etiquette, but with little enthusiasm, the master invited them to spend a moment freshening up in his house. He, too, was tired of waiting and irritated to have government agents poking their noses in his affairs.

The peasants had to keep waiting for as long as these niceties took. At last, Abdullah came out of the house and told them to group themselves by family and stand in rows. Most of them bickered about being first outside the master's door. Sardar was quite prepared to be pushed to the back, but Talla demonstrated she could be authoritative and managed to put herself first in line: her husband had livestock, and no one leaves livestock untended for a whole day! She called Sardar over to join her. She stood bolt upright, she was tall, the tallest woman in the village. Sardar watched her grow from year to year and wondered when she would stop. The hem of her chador kept rising higher, her ankles were now clearly visible as well as her bare feet in their worn shoes.

Talla stood her ground determinedly outside the master's house. It was not so much the place itself that mattered, but the fact she had secured it. She needed to drive out the uncertainty that had lingered in her heart since she came to the Tehran region, and she could do this by asserting herself, by achieving just one thing, one place. On the other hand, as soon as she had to step through the front door to the master's house, all her combative resolve evaporated. She huddled behind Sardar and let him go through the door first. But there was nothing important about Sardar as far as the men from the government were concerned. They were exasperated by villages full of reticent peasants who simply did not understand the concept of registration or a family name, and, worse, knew neither their age nor their date of birth. Identities had to be invented for them: "Where are you from?—From Khorasan.— I'll put Khorasani as your family name." Not everyone agreed with this, some wanted to forget the past and now thought of themselves as Tehranis. Others could not decide. "Well, what was your father's work?" And so on.

In Sardar's case, things were relatively simple: His name was Sardar Amir, his first name was Sardar and his father's name was Amir. That was the name he went by at home, and here, too.

"All right, then, Sardar Amir . . . place of birth?"

"Ghamsar in Kashan."

"Date of birth?"

"Maybe twenty-four years ago."

"Right, we'll go with twenty-four."

Then came Talla's turn, and she was still silent beneath her chador and *roubandeh*. Sardar spoke for his wife:

"Put Amir for her too," he said, although Talla protested later. "And she's about sixteen, born in Ghamsar in Kashan."

"Good."

They were given two sheets of paper, but neither of them could read so they did not know which was Sardar's and which Talla's. Due to this uncertainty they always kept the two together.

And that was how, a few years before Bahram's birth, his father had chosen the name of his family and all his progeny . . .

That is how Sardar arrived in Davoudieh with a family name, an identity card, and the right to vote, acquired thanks to the constitutional revolution. And like all men, by royal decree, he wore a European-style jacket and the distinctive peaked cap that Iranians named a "Pahlavi hat" after their new king. But he would not be voting in the biennial legislative elections that the master never fails to tell the villagers about, letting them know where the nearest polling stations are. Not because he, Sardar, knows that Reza Shah has brought an end to political parties and chooses his congressmen in advance, but because he believes this sort of thing belongs to another world far removed from his own. He is illiterate, and feels there is a clear boundary between himself and those who can read and write. If and when newspapers come into his hands, he uses them as wrapping. And all he remembers of them are the few photographs, which he studies slowly and carefully. He is often captivated and invents a story for each photograph, thinking, That must be what it is. Sometimes he is so convinced by his account that he relates it to Talla as if it were certified fact. Most people do more or less the same thing, apart from the masters, and even some of them: Almost everyone here is illiterate.

The only place where Sardar might hear talk of national affairs is the mosque. But he does not go to the mosque. He believes in God and the Prophet, and has faith in Islam, and that is enough for him. Sardar was a hunting man in Ghamsar, he is a shepherd in Tehran; solitary men make do without intermediaries when it comes to God.

Sardar is far above gatherings of men. He has always contemplated life from high up in the mountains in Ghamsar or from the hills in Shemiran. By looking from such a great height, he has a sense of how small men are. He knows that poverty is not the root of destitution, but greed. The distance he maintains with other people is not the same as Talla's. It is not born of fear but of dissent and caution. Fortunately, he does not live in the shadow of a master who, like all masters, has the power to tell the peasants how to cast their votes. Inhabitants of the Armenian village vote for representatives of their religious denomination; they would never ask a Muslim to vote for a non-Muslim.

As for Talla, she would never dream that she might be able to intervene in any way in national affairs. She would find the very idea as grotesque as blasphemy. Luckily, no one has told her about the right to vote, nor ever will, because it would make her angry, and she has no interest in women's rights. She gets what she wants, either by force of will or by the power of her tears. And what she wants never flies so high that she has to go and fight her case before important men. Talla is mistress of her home, in her small room in the Armenian village, with her worldly goods that fit in one simple bundle and her husband whom she has in the palm of her hand.

Two years after Bahram was born, his parents buy a little plot of development land in Gholhak, under Reza Shah's jurisdiction. And they become the owners of a house and a sheepfold surrounded by a large garden.

Eighteen years earlier, Sardar had sold his land and his rifle for five tomans. Starting with those five tomans, he has now bought a house with an upper floor, surrounded by a huge garden. He has worked tirelessly, without ever complaining. Not that he is to be pitied; he has always had enough food, and enough of his tobacco to smoke. His wife, the only living creature that matters to him, has always been by his side, and now so is his son. Nothing else—beautiful clothes, a car—has ever featured in his dreams. He sees them pass by like pretty pictures, like stars in the sky. And who in their right mind would dream of having a star in their pocket? Anyway, however rich he may be, a peasant is nothing compared to a master, compared to a nobleman. It is these masters who carry the world, who make decisions and issue orders. They may sometimes be frightening, but just having them there is often reassuring. Sardar would not want to make decisions for other people, not for anything in the world. If he were offered the opportunity, what would he decide? Nothing. Everything is right as it is: the land, the flock, water, tobacco. Sardar feels no resentment, frustration, unachievable longing, or hatred. Nothing that would motivate him to make decisions for other people, to command or change the world. And in order for things to continue as they are now, the differences must stay the same, so he leaves them as they are.

The only thing that occasionally saddens him is Talla's changeable moods, her lively personality. He would like his wife to be softer, more gentle, not so quick-tempered; he would like her always to get up on the right side of the bed. He wishes she were the same every evening, that he could step over the threshold of his house without wondering what her first words will be, the first expression on her face. But it's not important; he manages. What matters is that she's there, she lies down beside him every evening and he sees her face every morning. His thirst for her, which grew stronger every day in the three years he waited to touch her, will never die.

And Talla, too, has worked from dawn to dusk, because she wanted a home of their own. Even the birth of their son did nothing to change that. And yet that birth was a miracle. Talla kept saying that if she did not conceive again after her first son died, then it was Sardar's fault, because he had thrown water over a yellow cat. And if you throw water over a yellow cat, the cat curses you and you will never have children.

From the moment he was born, she cosseted her miracle baby. She put him to the breast and gave him her milk till he was two years old, because she so needed to feel his little body thrive. But without ever neglecting her chores. She carried him on her back wherever she went. Delivering milk and cheese, going to the bread oven. And even when she was driving the sheep, all through their travels, heading south of Tehran in winter and back to Shemiran in summer.

But the most important thing was to own their own home, as they had planned one summer night on a hillside, right here in Shemiran. And now they do.

Their union has stayed the course, for the best and against all the odds.

III
MAHINE,
A WOMAN'S PLEASURE

T ell me why we left Ghamsar and came here and worked like mules all these years to achieve only half of what you had back there: a house and a few animals! We don't even have any land here. The plot you sold in Ghamsar was much bigger than this little bit of garden."

Sardar says nothing as he looks at Talla's face, its skin burnished by the passing years, seared by the sun and the cold. Only in the folds of her wrinkles is there still a hint of the original color. But in contrast to her dark skin, her green eyes are even more piercing, challenging, and alluring. He loves this fatally untamed woman. He puts his hand on hers and strokes it slowly, his own calloused skin catching on the rough surface of her hand. There is nothing unpleasant about this. Quite the opposite, they would know each other by touch even with their eyes closed. Besides, Sardar loves being the only one to know that hiding beneath this apparently rustic exterior are breasts, thighs, and a stomach that, sheltered from the sun and wind, are still as soft as on their wedding night.

"Why? Firstly, to be proud that we had the courage to leave. Secondly, so that your son—my son—and your son's son, and his son could know the world. Ghamsar is a land hemmed in by mountains. A paradise and a prison. The men and women who live there are happy to know nothing of the world on the far side of the mountains. I wanted to see that world, I wanted to live beyond the mountains. And even if I can't share in all this wealth, my son shall. I'm sure of that."

For fear of looking cowardly, he would tell her his other reason for leaving only when disaster struck. In 1335 a terrible flood destroyed a large swath of Ghamsar, not for the first time. Freighted with mud and rock, the floodwaters tumbled down the mountain, swallowing everything along the banks of the river, including the house in which Sardar was born, and its inhabitants. First there was a roaring sound and the light changed, then a tower of water as tall as the mountain bore down on Ghamsar. Suddenly, with no warning. In the time it took to grasp what was happening, the time it took to freeze incredulously, before there was even time for horror, it swept everything away.

While houses toppled into the river, while uprooted trees tore up others in their path, and the clear water became more and more of a black chaos loaded with people, animals, and belongings, those who were not in its path cried: "*Ya ghamar-e bani hashem!*"

When calm was restored at last, rose petals floated on the water in the great chasm where the river had once flowed.

A nd so the Amir family settles in Gholdhak, a village in Shemiran to the north of Davoudieh; a place famous for its seven *qanats*, underground irrigation channels. The most famous of them served Gholhak's elite summer residences, belonging to the British ambassador and the aristocrat Ghavam el-Saltaneh, who was five times prime minister, under both the Qajar and the Pahlavi.

Talla would loathe herself for bowing and scraping to masters, but in Gholhak she bows admiringly before aristocrats. Unlike masters, they are not threatening, merely eminent. They are quite a sight in their European clothes with their heads held high and their eyes turned to the horizon, apparently not even aware of peasants. And of course indifference is far more alluring than contempt.

At the feet of this nobility in Gholhak, surrounded by quiet and gardens, life naturally becomes so pleasant that it is hard to believe it has ever been otherwise. Gone is the bustle of men and animals, the endless coming and going in the master's yard, and the grueling proximity with other tenants. And no more master, ever!

In Gholhak they can finally set up home. Sardar stops keeping his sheep out on the hills. He has considerably reduced his flock in order to buy the house, and now keeps his sheep in his own stabling. He also builds a proper chicken coop in his garden. It is now Talla who looks after the animals and the house, and Sardar devotes his time to cultivating the land he still rents from the master in the Armenian village. And in the great wilderness around their house Bahram plays with his friend Ali-Agha, son of Mahtab-Khanoum, Gholhak's midwife and Talla's only friend. There are just two houses in this part of the village: Talla and Sardar's and the one belonging to Mahtab-Khanoum and her husband Mirza, Gholak's water master. Huddled within their own walls, they stand facing each other. And behind those walls, Talla is free at last to live and work without her chador. For fifteen years she removed her chador only inside the cramped rooms they rented, or occasionally alone on the plain, brief moments stolen from that life of sheltering from others' eyes. She now spends most of her time working in her garden without her chador or *roubandeh*. And sometimes she has fun climbing her mulberry tree and going up onto the roof of her house, or playing with her son in her garden. And her skin, which saw no sunlight for all those years, has visibly darkened, her complexion becoming the same as Sardar's, and they agree that happiness is a color.

They had only just started enjoying these private freedoms when women's emancipation was enshrined in law. Reza Shah forbade the wearing of chadors, and instructed police officers to strip them from women who braved the new law. Pandemonium. Women shut themselves away at home, men barricaded them in. No one in the lower ranks of society understood the law. It struck them as a punishment. "What business is it of the king's to rip chadors off old ladies in the street? What sort of king is he, denying his people's wishes?" But Reza Shah was powerful and authoritarian, and people were afraid of him. On the other hand, the law was welcomed by many who had already stopped wearing the chador in private, the wives and daughters of men who lived in the twentieth century and not the Middle Ages, as they themselves would see it. In the higher echelons of society, women changed overnight, coming out into the open without chadors, in European clothes, wearing hats, long dresses, and highheeled shoes. There were a few, particularly in rural areas, who wanted to defy the law but had no choice: Reza Shah had commanded it; this was the Reza Shahi era and his word must be obeyed on pain of death. They obeyed. Even Tehran's street sweepers, like all the city's lowly workers, were forced to stroll along the boulevards with their wives unveiled.

In the streets of Gholhak the wives of noblemen and eminent figures suddenly emerged from their houses without chadors. People here were used to seeing European women wearing hats; but they were Farangis, infidels from different lands and of different faiths. They were classified almost in the same category as djinns and peris, creatures from beyond time, beyond the known world. They appeared and disappeared before you could be sure you had seen them properly. But Iranian women were their kind, they were Muslims and real.

Some women stayed cloistered indoors until necessity forced them outside. Others did not emerge until many years later, when the law fell into obsolescence. These women simply could not imagine showing themselves without their chador to men in the street, and neither could their husbands countenance it. Given the choice between going to hell and staying shut away at home, they chose or were constrained to stay at home.

Mirza did not disguise his anger: "This started with the royal decree about uniform. The Shah ordered all men to wear peaked caps and European suits. We had to abandon our tunics and belts for a shirt and jacket. The more 'advanced' even added a false collar and a tie. Most of us kept to the jacket and cap, we grumbled but we had to obey. And now look, he's taken off women's chadors . . .

"People knew this would happen, they knew in Tehran. There were protests, and even demonstration in Meshed. Well, the rebels were hounded even inside Imam Reza's sanctuary. Can you imagine? There is nowhere in the country more sacred than Imam Reza's sanctuary in Meshed!" Mirza exclaimed to Sardar, then he pointed indignantly to the heavens as he added, "I take God as my witness, my wife will stay at home. Women will have their babies without her. I won't let Mahtab-Khanoum onto the street without her chador—never!"

Talla was among those who resisted by staying at home. She, who was so active and who busied around the neighborhood from morning to evening, stayed closeted within her garden walls. Neither she nor Sardar could contemplate her showing herself in the street without a chador. It had been different in Ghamsar, but from the moment she went beyond the mountain she had worn the chador, and she had not removed it in public since. The chador was the costume of her new life. And she had now lived longer with it than without it. To Talla, wearing the chador was not only a question of religion, it was her refuge, a barrier between herself and other people. Hidden like this, she was safe. If she was forced to remove it, her private sanctuary would be violated. Quite apart from her respect for the custom that forbade her showing her hair to men, she found the chador reassuring, like a mother's womb, protective and enveloping. Since leaving Ghamsar, this piece of fabric had put a veil between her and this untrustworthy world, making it less real, less aggressive.

Talla was not a child of the city, and was not afraid of men; as a girl she had wandered her village without a chador. Here, she was not protecting herself from men's eyes but from life's unknowns. Removing her chador meant being part of the real world with no protection. The spell would be broken and she would be vulnerable. But at the same time, there was an element of exorcism in this enforced removal. What if she had come full circle? What if this new world had accepted her, had agreed to her presence, and there was now no danger of it swallowing her up in a fit of temper?

Days went by and Talla grew bored. Worse than this, her work was getting behind. Sardar could not do everything. If she did not start making her deliveries again, then the milk, yogurt, and cheese would spoil. She had to do something. Pacing like a caged lion, Talla seethed and muttered to herself. She wanted to delay the decision; the idea of living without the veil was maturing, although she would have hated to admit it.

For years Talla would relate the tale of this intolerable power struggle between a peasant woman and the state:

"Reza Shah banned the chador, women were no longer allowed to wear it. Everyone was afraid of Reza Shah in those days, they said he had thieves torn limb from limb, that he'd massacred men even inside Imam Reza's sanctuary in Meshed. So when he banned the chador I stayed at home for a long time. Sardar delivered my fresh products for two weeks, but he couldn't do everything, working the land and doing deliveries, so our produce was rotting and I had to throw things away, more and more every day. It broke my heart emptying out whole pails of milk and cream. It brought tears to my eyes. One day I was so angry I decided to go and deliver the eggs myself, wearing my chador and my *roubandeh*! I delivered everything without any trouble but on the way back a policeman stopped me and asked: 'Don't you know the chador has been banned?'

"'You have no respect for God or the Prophet,' I replied. 'You've all become unbelievers.'

"He was angry, called me every name under the sun, and tried to pull off my chador. I fought back and my chador tore but he didn't manage to remove it. I told him he was the son of a dog, and started running away. I was glad I'd told him what had been eating away at me for weeks. He ran after me but I was faster than him. With his uniform, his hat, and his stick, he had trouble catching up with me. I could hear him shouting behind me:

"'You've insulted a state policeman, I'll have you put in prison!'

"I turned onto my street and reached my house, but didn't have time to get out my key to open the door. So I took off my chador and my *roubandeh*, slung them over the garden wall, and quickly sat myself down outside the front door. When he eventually reached me he asked:

"'Where did the woman with the torn chador go?'

"'She went that way.'

"He thanked me and set off again. I was saved!"

Every time Talla told this story she roared with laughter and repeated that he was a "son of a dog!"

As she sat outside her door that day, when the policeman had run on and she was feeling pleased with herself, Talla tilted her head to the sky and for the first time felt the sun's caress on her face outside the wall of her house and not behind it; and it had a profound effect on her, she felt a childlike happiness, it made her want to squeal for joy, as she used to back in Ghamsar over the most trifling thing. But she did not cry out, she lowered her head and looked away into the distance with a tiny smile playing in the corners of her mouth. She looked at what she was wearing: leggings beneath an ankle-length tunic, and a large scarf over her head, held with a pin under her chin. She was out on the street with no chador or *roubandeh* . . . and she was afraid of nothing.

But she did not mention this when she told the story, perhaps because it is better for the sin to be laid at Reza Shah's door.

B ahram was six when Talla handed him a leather satchel and said, "You're going to school tomorrow."
"But why?"
"You're going to learn to read and write, you're going to be what they call literate."
Reza Shah had introduced free, compulsory public schools.
This was the only initiative of his—apart from the ban on chadors—that the Amir family heard about or that tangibly affected them. They knew nothing of any of the others: they read no newspapers, had no official obligations to fulfill, and did not travel, not even into Tehran, not even to the local mosque. The construction of Iran's railways, its first power station, its 24,000 civil servants, its legal system, and even the confiscation of religious institutions' assets did not disrupt their day-to-day lives in any way.

But they knew Bahram had to go to school.

The following morning, on the first day of autumn, Talla gave Bahram the empty satchel after breakfast and recited a surah from the Koran. Then she blew in his face, circling her mouth around him so that her breath was blessed and would cover all of his face. Sardar, who usually headed off to the field early, had hung back. He had made a show of being busy in the garden with tools to mend and things to put away. Talla knew why he was still hovering, he wanted to see his son go off to school, so she pretended not to notice him.

When Talla reached for Bahram's hand to take him to

school, Sardar said, "May God watch over you!" and he felt happiness deep in his heart. Sardar's thoughts were simple and could always be expressed in one sentence: "That's another reason I came to Tehran" or "My son goes to school." Then he shook his head, sighed, brought his hand to his eyes, and wiped away the beginnings of tears.

T he school has only one classroom and is set up in the garden of a scholarly Gholhak dignitary, in a building he lends to the state. As is the case all over Iran, makeshift classrooms are being used until the local school has been built.

Talla leaves Bahram outside the school and says, "Go on," and Bahram heads off alone in the direction his mother points.

In the garden there are children of all ages waiting, watched over by a supervisor who does not have to use his authority this first day: They all look a little baffled and are in no mood for mischief. Some know each other and are happy to see each other. Bahram spots his neighbor and friend, Ali-Agha, and runs over to hug him, reassured not to be facing the fray alone.

The schoolmistress appears out of nowhere—pretty, modern, wearing a skirt—and Bahram is delighted when he sees her. She ushers the children into the classroom, girls and boys together. The youngest are six, the oldest twelve or thirteen. The building is a storehouse that must have been emptied hastily to make room for benches and chairs. The children have no desks, and there is only just enough room for them all to sit and write on their laps. The teacher has a desk and her own chair.

A scant four years after the chador was banned, there she sits in her western-style dress with her curly hair and bare arms clearly visible, as are her legs and heeled shoes under the table.

A photograph of Reza Shah hangs on the wall, facing the

children. Bahram does not recognize this man with his moustache and military uniform. He has seen postcards before, and
pictures in the newspapers, but never a life-size portrait. From
this very first day, Bahram refuses to sit down, frightened to
face the picture of Reza Shah with his severe expression. He
cannot understand why the man is looking at him alone.
Clutching his satchel in one arm, he crouches under the
teacher's desk, and there he means to stay. The teacher, whom
the children know as Mrs. Tabatabai but address shyly as
"Miss," is amused and eventually agrees to let him stay there.

Every day, from eight in the morning till school finishes at
noon, Bahram stays close to his teacher's legs, and over time he
becomes her protégé. She clucks over him like a hen with her
egg, and when he is close to her he is always in good spirits. If
he needs to see the blackboard, the teacher makes him come
out of his hiding place, and he sits on a shelf along the wall.

"Do you love me?" she asks him one day.

"Yes, I do," Bahram replies.

She sometimes asks him to fetch something from her house
near Gholhak's old village. Bahram hurries off and returns in
record time. He runs fast, very fast, but for now his teacher is
alone in marveling at this unusual ability.

Time goes by with him under the desk, on his shelf, or out
in the garden. Around ten o'clock one morning when they are
having a lesson outside, Ali-Agha's father comes to collect his
son and take him to the hammam. Mirza arrives discreetly and
bows a couple of times to the teacher and then, head lowered,
asks permission to take his son to the hammam. She grants her
permission, and Ali-Agha stands up and follows his father.
Bahram watches them leave and when they are about to disap-
pear at the bottom of the garden he jumps to his feet and runs
to catch up with them. He leaps over the other pupils, knocks
over a chair, falls, picks himself up, and races on. The teacher
calls him but has no success: Off he flies and is gone for the day.

"I thought you loved me!" she says reproachfully the following day.

"I do."

"Then why did you leave? Why didn't you come back when I called?"

"Ali-Agha's my friend," Bahram replied simply.

"So do you love him more than me?"

"No."

"I'm not sure I believe you," she cajoles.

"Well, I came back today so that means I love you. I wanted to check they were going to the hammam. Because in my house we go to the hammam on Fridays, when there's no school."

"You won't do it again will you?"

"No."

Before he turned six, Bahram would go to the hammam with his mother, among women. This lasted until they started complaining: "He's a big boy now, and he's seeing us naked," they said, adding with shocked astonishment, "he won't stop staring between our legs." From then on Bahram had to go to the hammam with his father who, unlike his mother, would pour scalding water over his head to "get the impurities out of your skin," and Bahram would scream that it was burning him.

The water for the hammam came from the *qanat* for the British ambassador's summer residence. A thick layer of grease and dirt hung over the top of the big pool. A gang of local reprobates, who liked showing off their muscles and tattoos at the hammam, messed around, sucking the scum into their mouths and blowing it over their friends. Men washed in the pool and then rinsed themselves down with clean water from a tap. There were small rooms arranged around the pool, and some men would hide behind their yellowish curtains and apply hair-removal cream. The tattooed youths who skulked off into these dark rooms frightened Bahram.

"Those men are interested in little boys," his father warned him, "they have bad thoughts in their heads."

Bahram wondered what they could possibly get up to in those confined spaces, and missed the days spent at the hammam with women.

He was eight by the time the hammam was fitted with showers. Sardar now paid a few extra coins and offered his son a shower so he no longer had to wash in that filthy water.

When he arrived home from school at noon one day, Bahram came across Talla in the garden making her yogurt: She had made great bowlfuls of it, and she let Bahram taste it.

"Will you give me a pail of it for my teacher?" he asked. "She'll really like it."

He set off with his pail of yogurt and for once he did not run, but he swung his head from left to right as he walked so that he felt he was going quickly while he held the pail steady. He came to the teacher's front door and rapped three times with the door knocker. The maid opened the door and when he asked to see her mistress, she invited him into the living room. The door was open so Bahram stepped in and, to his surprise, he saw his teacher sitting next to a man and drinking soup.

"Hello," he said. "I've brought you some yogurt my mother made."

His teacher smiled and stood up to greet him, but Bahram put down the pail, muttered a "goodbye," and ran off.

"Bahram, Bahram, wait!" his teacher called, but he did not turn back.

At school the next day Bahram sat on the bench like the other pupils for the first time.

"What's the matter?" his teacher asked him at the end of lessons. "Is something wrong?"

"Yes, something's wrong."

"What is it?"

"You were sitting with a man yesterday," he said quietly.

"Yes, he's my husband."

"You shouldn't have!"

"What?" she asked.

"You shouldn't have!"

"Go away, you naughty boy," the teacher said, shoving him toward the door irritably.

Bahram headed for the door but she caught up with him, put her arms around him and kissed his cheek.

"Now go," she said.

He slipped outside and sat on the steps. The teacher came out, too, and walked past him without turning around.

When Bahram remembered this incident later, he was reminded of another teacher who went on to become a film actress. Perhaps it was the same woman.

Bahram did not go back to school after that, and he persuaded Ali-Agha not to either. They went to the mulberry garden in Toutestan, to the north of Gholhak, a place that was usually deserted. They would play on the banks of the stream that cut through the garden and then go home at noon . . . until the day when Sangchine, the school's caretaker, caught them by this stream.

"Hey! What are you doing here?"

They fled and never went back to Toutestan. Nor to school: They were only in preliminary classes, and their parents felt that three months of school was plenty to start with.

They spent the rest of the year wandering around the area. They often went to Davoudieh's ice pit, which fascinated them because it was the local attraction and they had heard that long ago a frozen body was found in it.

This ice pit had a wall at least fifty feet high and well over six feet thick, erected facing the northern mountains. The cold wind blowing off the mountains hit the wall and chilled it. At the foot of the northern side of the wall a three-foot-deep ditch had been dug. On winter evenings this was filled with water which froze overnight, and in the morning men in rubber boots would climb down into the ditch, gather the ice, and pass it through a gap in the wall. On the southern side was another ditch at least thirty feet deep and thirty feet wide. The ice accumulated in this second pit was covered with straw all through the winter. In summer, this muddy ice riddled with grass stalks was sold locally or delivered by truck to cafes and eateries in Tehran.

When modern refrigerators came along they would be called "ice pits" in Iran.

Sardar no longer has a flock of sheep to drive over Gholhak's hills but he still wanders the hills alone. For the pleasure of it, and because he needs to be high up to feel alive.

When he arrives home one summer evening in 1319, he opens up his bag in front of Talla, and takes out a freshly killed rabbit.

"You've had fun playing the hunter again," she says. "What are we going to do with it?"

"I don't know but isn't it beautiful? It took me a while to catch it. It wore me out, but I'm glad I haven't lost the touch."

"I think the Farangi eat them."

Talla knows that foreigners eat rabbits, a servant reported this bizarre fact—one among so many. There happens to be a German diplomat and his family living very nearby. Holding the rabbit up by its hind legs, she calls her son and shows it to him.

"Go to the Germans' house and sell them this rabbit. Take whatever they give you for it."

Bahram sets off at a run. There is nothing to check a runner's speed on the plain; it is vast and man is light-footed. But Bahram has more than other people in his legs, a gift, a will, something aided and abetted by open terrain. He runs with the rabbit at arm's length, its head bobbing rhythmically.

The rusted gate to the Germans' residence stands ajar. As Bahram pushes it open with his free hand, he hears on the cool evening breeze the muted music of a gramophone mingling with the sounds of splashing water and women's voices. Trees block his view, allowing only diffuse light through. Bahram walks a few paces up the drive, then cuts through the trees toward the light. On the far side he sees men in trunks and women in swimming costumes, some sitting around a pool, others in the water. What a strange sight! He is seven years old and has already seen naked women at the hammam, but nearly naked women and men in underwear, together, in the same place, looking happy and not embarrassed—it can't be, or it's just a dream. Astonished, he avidly watches every detail, every move of this fantastical gathering. As he slowly gets used to the spectacle he notices that some of the women have golden hair that glows in the lamplight, and that their skin is white as snow. He sees one woman in the water laughing and playing with one of the men, putting her arm around his neck and kissing his cheek. The man strokes her back. How intoxicating!

One of the Farangis spots him and calls him over. Bahram remembers why he is here and walks over to the man with a smile. Having had an opportunity to watch them, he can give some impression of familiarity, as if he is in on their secrets. He feels the German will have no choice but to buy the rabbit at a good price.

"Would you like a rabbit?" he asks loudly, brandishing it toward the man.

"Mahmoud!" the German cries, turning toward the residence.

While they wait for Mahmoud to arrive, the German gesticulates wildly at Bahram who gathers the man is not interested in his rabbit, so he goes around all the others, offering the rabbit. Some of them laugh, others looked disgusted, especially the women. An elderly man appears and the German asks him, in rudimentary Persian, to get rid of the boy. Bahram calls him "sir" and explains that he only wants to sell his rabbit and he knows Farangis eat rabbit, he knows they do. The old man tells him these particular ones do not, and pushes him toward the gates. And that is where the dream comes to an end.

Bahram goes home disappointed but happy. Disappointed because he would have liked them to buy his rabbit so he could go back on the pretext of selling them other things. And happy because he has seen what he has seen. That evening he and his family climb up onto the roof to sleep in the cooler air and, lying there beneath Shemiran's starry sky, Bahram dreams of those German women with their white skin and golden hair.

Rumor had it that Reza Shah was turning cemeteries into schools, so Gholhak's school would be built on the plot of the old cemetery. The first schoolchildren to use it would see the ground swell up in places and ooze an oily substance—humors from decomposing bodies, people said.

Bahram was in the first-year group to go through this compulsory, mixed primary school that came to be known as "Djam" and promised to be prestigious. It had six classes from first grade through sixth grade, an amphitheater, a large yard, a swimming pool, a house for the headmaster, and another for the janitor, as well as sports fields and equipment for volleyball, soccer, basketball, pole-vaulting . . .

All the pupils wore uniforms: a gray dress with a Peter Pan collar for the girls and a gray suit with a white shirt for the boys.

That first year, they were of mixed ages and from every sort of background, the destitute and the well-to-do. The state school had to be open to absolutely everyone; it would not have been right to take only seven-year-olds and forsake older children, so they took all the local children over seven.

The school's headmaster—"may he rest in peace," Bahram would later say whenever he mentioned his name—was an imposing character who ran his own little world with a firm hand. Under his authority were several teachers, both men and women, including his own wife. In each class the teacher would appoint a prefect to keep an eye on the other pupils when he or she was out of the room, and to report any disruptions. There were severe punishments, especially the *falak,* when the pupil lay full length with his or her legs attached firmly to a wooden stick that one teacher held up while another beat the soles of the wrongdoer's feet. The beating itself hurt but the worst of it was having to walk afterward . . .

The teacher, the most powerful person in the world after the headmaster, stood with his hands behind his back, dictating:

"Hossein goes to school . . . Hossein's mother does the washing . . . Hossein's father is a farmer . . . "

Bahram wrote with a fountain pen—known as a "French pen"—that he dipped into an inkwell filled with Chinese ink and tiny pieces of fabric to act as a sponge.

Their schoolmaster also taught them that Iran is an ancient civilization and it had been bequeathed to them by great kings like Darius and Cyrus who forged an empire whose glory knows no end. Bahram believed everything his teacher said.

On the very first day of school, the teacher noticed that Bahram wrote with his left hand, which, according to him, went against the laws of nature. He rapped Bahram across the hand with his metal ruler: "We write with the right hand." Bahram found it very difficult, but the beatings eventually had their effect. He took to holding the pen in his right hand, blinking his eyes briefly, then writing. It was a habit that stayed with him his whole life: a tension, an irritation, a few blinks . . . For drawing and painting, though, he would continue using his left hand.

Luckily, all the hardships inflicted on him by his teacher paled in significance beside the joy he felt about his new pigeons. When he first went to school, his father gave him two, a male and a female. As soon as lessons were over, Bahram fled in a flash to get home to them.

Like all his friends, Bahram played the pigeon game, which consisted in making your pigeon fly higher than everyone else's to win the round. This was called the "pigeon game" but also "the love game," and "pigeon players" were also known as "lovers."

"There are some regions in Iran where they've built towers for their pigeons," his father told him. "Very tall towers with thousands of alcoves, each alcove houses two birds, imagine how many pigeons that is . . . They're bred for their droppings, they're a good fertilizer, very rich . . . "

From that moment on, Bahram dreamed of having a pigeon tower in his garden.

While Bahram's future was being nurtured at Djam School, something wonderful came into Sardar's life: radio. The first time Sardar heard a radio, it was like a divine sound coming out of a box, a sound from paradise—it was music. He had never heard an orchestra play music before. He had occasionally heard a flute, a peasant song, popular music played at weddings, but this sound was . . . Sardar had no words to describe what he was hearing so he simply told Talla, "It's beautiful." This was at Gholhak's police station some time after Radio Tehran had been set up. Sardar looked at the box and was not afraid of it; he even went over and touched it and asked how it worked. He was told that the sound was sent from the sky and landed in the box. "Allahu Akbar," he murmured and stood puzzling for a moment, but then what did it matter how it worked! He realized that once they had electricity in their house, he could buy a radio of his own, take it home, and listen to it every day. Happy with this, he smiled and nodded his head as he announced, "We'll wait for the electricity, then."

For some time now a black cat had been covetously eyeing the Amirs' chicken coop, a stubborn cat who took no notice of Talla's threats. Then one day Sardar caught him in the act: The cat was walking surreptitiously toward the henhouse, one paw after another, unaware that Sardar was following him slowly and silently, the perfect huntsman. When Sardar caught up with the cat, he drew out his knife and cut off its tail. The cat wailed, leapt over the wall, and was never seen again.

Talla saw this incident as a sign and remembered a promise she had made to God to make a pilgrimage to Shah-Abdol-Azim if Bahram reached the age of six. She felt it was high time she fulfilled this promise. Sardar would not come with her; he would have liked to, but had to look after the house and the animals. Each to his or her own duties.

Very early one Friday morning, Talla puts a few provisions into a bundle, fills a gourd with water, hides her money in a tightly knotted fold of her scarf, takes Bahram's hand, and sets off on this adventure.

They catch the bus to Tehran—the first time Talla has taken a bus. Oh my! If it weren't for the love of God, she would never have set foot in one of the things. She clings to her seat all the way to the Shemiran Gate, which, with its columns and Persian tiles like the gates to a palace in the middle of nowhere, finally announces they have reached Tehran. The city Talla has never visited. Sardar, for some mysterious reason, had always said it wasn't for them and they mustn't tempt the devil. Even though Talla had put less stock in Sardar's words since Bahram was born, she now remembers his enigmatic pronouncements and wonders whether she is outside the majestic gates of hell. When she returns to Gholhak, this trip will earn her universal respect: It takes courage to travel so far without your husband. But for now, she grips Bahram's hand and he tries desperately to break away, but there is nothing for it, she is frightened. What if the devil himself was waiting for them on the other side! For a moment she even considers turning back. But then what could she tell God? She looks around her, but the other passengers on the bus don't look frightened. Granted, they're all men; there isn't a single other woman among them. But still. Well. It has to be done, for the love of God, it has to be done.

So this is Tehran: cars, horse-drawn carts, bicycles, pedestrians, policemen, buildings, wide avenues . . . the most beautiful, the most impressive thing is the vast Toup-Khaneh Square surrounded by buildings with thousands of balconies and adorned with ponds, fountains, flowers, and lampposts. And the city is teeming with people. Women in hats, high-heeled shoes, and silk stockings; headdresses in folded fabric, turbans of satin, of twisted velvet; hats decorated with feathers or freshly picked flowers. Other women go bareheaded. And men in homburgs, and collars and ties, some even have coats with fur collars. Over there a porter carrying buckets of yogurt piled up on his head. And suddenly a donkey nonchalantly crossing in front of the bus. And also some normal people like Talla, or Sardar: women in scarves and full robes over leggings and men in worn, ill-fitting jackets, pants that are too big or too short, with their heads uncovered or wearing the hat decreed by Reza Shah. Tehran is too big, too beautiful, extravagant, outlandish, strange . . .

Their journey across the capital ends at Khorasan Gate,

where they are to catch the smoking engine at a station that goes by the French name of "Gare machine" because it was a French engineer who secured the first railway concession from Naser al-Din Shah Qajar in 1261, linking Tehran to Shahr-e Rey. The engineer thought he would be transporting the quantities of pilgrims heading for Shah-Abdol-Azim's mausoleum. No one ever knows why some wonderful ideas fail to take, just as the yogurt sometimes fails to take in Talla's expert hands. "The smoking engine," as it is known here, is a steam train that drew crowds for a while without ever achieving its anticipated success. The passengers stand in an open-sided carriage. Bahram is thrilled to be taking the smoking engine but Talla is a little disoriented—too many novelties for one day. When the train sets off, children race after it, throwing pebbles. Bahram watches them with delight: he's better than them, he's inside and they're outside.

The train stops by the Shah-Abdol-Azim sanctuary in Shahr-e Rey. When Talla lived in Shahr-e Rey she never had an opportunity to come here. She and Sardar discussed it and thought about making the trip but it never happened, they never had the time. What splendor! Shah-Abdol-Azim was a descendant of the Imam Hassan, and his tomb has two magnificent minarets reaching up toward the sky, and three domes, one of which is golden. Inside are a myriad of mirrors reflecting each other into infinity and reflecting the thousands of tears shed by pilgrims. Bahram is fascinated by so much beauty combined with the ecstatic state his mother is in as she weeps helplessly for joy. Talla strokes the walls of the tomb several times and then smooths her now blessed hand over Bahram's face. Her rough skin chafes his face, leaving him in doubt that it is his mother's hand. That abrasive feel, the mark of her motherhood, loving and harsh.

They leave the sanctuary exhausted. Talla drops to the ground in the corner and pretends to die. This has become a habit of hers, a macabre joke she indulges in more and more frequently with Bahram now that he is growing up and has started trying to avoid her invasive love. Talla still wants her son in her belly or clamped to her breast, wants him there now and forever. Talla is compulsively possessive about everything, and most of all about her son. So she plays this part well, and it torments Bahram. Even though he knows from experience it is an act, he cannot help panicking. There is always some doubt. What if this time she really died?

Bahram runs over to the fountain, realizes he has nothing to carry water, asks someone for a bowl, comes back with the water, and tips some over Talla's face, then tries to get her to drink some and after a while—which feels like an eternity to him—she pretends to come back to life. Bahram is reassured but doubly exhausted now.

They take the smoking engine back, then the bus, and reach Gholhak after nightfall.

Sardar is sitting waiting for them by the side of the road, next to their garden door. It is the first time he has been at home without them. It is late, Tehran and Shar-e Rey are far away, and the roads dangerous. Whatever made him let them go on their own? He should have paid for a neighbor to go with them. His thoughts are very dark this evening. What if something's happened to them, what if they don't come back, or have been killed in an accident, what would he do all alone on this earth? Everything suddenly loses all meaning. His whole life, from Ghamsar to here, all those years of working to buy a house, land, animals. The milk, the yogurt, the butter . . . nothing would taste of anything or matter anymore. He would die, too, of grief. He has been sitting on this doorstep for three hours peering at the end of the road. And now here they are, in the distance he can see Talla's silhouette, and tears roll down his cheeks. He has been this happy to see her twice: once in Ghamsar when he came to claim her and now this evening.

And his son strolling behind her. Happiness blooms again. He'll give them everything, his whole life, it's nothing without them, he thinks. Then he gets to his feet, wipes away his tears, and goes back inside. He has already laid out the tablecloth, the bread and cheese. He draws water from the well. Everything is as it should be.

Electricity came to Sardar's house sooner than expected. A German who lived in Gholhak bought a generator for himself and—for a one-off fee of twenty tomans and a monthly subscription of one toman—he supplied other households with enough electricity for one light and a radio.

Almost before the line was installed Sardar hurried off to buy a radio. And, for the first time since their marriage, he made the decision without asking Talla's opinion. Filled with excitement, he plugged in his radio and settled himself beside it for the rest of his life.

As soon as he had finished his day's work he would sit by the radio, turn it on, light his pipe, and stay there enjoying both until the broadcasts finished. In those early years of Radio Tehran the signal was fairly mediocre, and Sardar spent more time turning the dials than listening to broadcasts. Still, he managed to receive an hour or two a day. Sometimes he came across programs in foreign languages, a rare curiosity for him, and he could listen to them at length. He had found what made him happy. He listened without commentary, and believed everything he heard. Everything, that is, that he could understand, because much of the meaning was lost on him. His preference was for music. It reached deep inside him and delighted him. He thought paradise must be filled with this music, that God was satisfied with his subjects and these were blessed times, which was why He was rewarding them with the gift of radio: the sound of paradise on earth. Sardar wanted to go to paradise. He wondered whether he had done anything in his life to hamper this, and could think of nothing. Sardar had faith in himself and in God.

On *Shahrivar* 3rd, 1320, a radio announcement about the mobilization of reservists sends shock waves through Gholhak. Iran is being invaded simultaneously by the Soviets in the north and the English in the south. The Iranians have hesitated to join the Allies in the war, their oil fields need protecting and a supply corridor for the Soviet army has to be established via the Arabian Sea.

Mahtab-Khanoum's eldest son Mohsen goes off to join the army, and his mother weeps in Talla's arms. Talla cries, too, because Iranian etiquette dictates that no one should cry alone.

In early *Shahrivar* 1320, at the foot of Gholhak's hill, where a few large jujube trees have grown up around a stream, four school friends are playing: Bahram, Ali-Agha, Siavosh, and Ghassem. They are all up in a jujube tree picking the fruit that they call "Chinese dates."

"I have the most!"

"No, I do! Look at them!"

"Whoever jumps out of the tree without dropping his dates is the winner!"

"I don't care about winning, I don't want to break a leg."

There on that tree, which is said to come from paradise and whose leaves are said to be a talisman against witchcraft, they should be safe from harm: The distant sound of other children laughing mingles with their own laughter, and the wind sifts playfully through the branches. They are happy. But there is suddenly a resounding explosion. They have never heard anything so loud. Panic-stricken, they obey their survival instinct: They jump from the tree and melt away. Except for Ali-Agha, who stays and picks up the dates his friends have left behind. Siavosh vanishes; Bahram and Ghassem run along the dry riverbed. They spot a bomber plane that has just dropped a bomb on the arms factory to the east of Gholhak.

They will never know whether it is a Russian plane or an English one, but it wheels around overhead, and Bahram and Ghassem think it is chasing them, that they are its next target. Bahram is now famous for his gift as a runner, but he slows regularly so as not to abandon his friend. He finds it impossible to go at the same speed as other people, so he constantly gets ahead and has to stop and wait for his friends. The two breathless boys take refuge under Gholhak's bridge. They watch the plane, peeping their shaven heads out and then hiding again, until it disappears on the horizon.

This marks the beginning of the black nights and chaotic days of the Allied offensive in Iran. In the Amir household on the evening after the bombing of Gholhak's factory, Talla fills a large pail of water and the three of them sit around it. The radio has told them: If a bomb is dropped they are to pour water over themselves. All their neighbors have done it too: All of Gholhak is sitting around buckets of water that evening.

Whole families of Tehranis arrive, talking of war, the Russians, the English, the bombing. Sardar, who left Ghamsar to get away from curses, starts to think that wherever you go the sky is the same color, and he who has the biggest roof has to sweep the most snow. In Ghamsar the invaders were bandits, in Tehran they are Farangi troops. But the people here seem to have no urge to flee into the mountain, they just say it will pass, that in Iran wars come to an end and invaders go back home, or become so Iranian themselves that they can no longer be distinguished from anyone else. As the saying goes: That, too, will pass. So Sardar eventually learns not to worry.

He gets himself organized, keeps himself busy, and thinks about protecting his animals and hiding his provisions.

Four days after leaving for war, Mohsen comes home: He has deserted like everyone else, even the officers vanished. That same day the Iranian government calls for a truce to negotiate their surrender. Nine infantry divisions along with the Iranian air force and navy have been annihilated in under a week. The oil fields and the trans-Iranian railway line have fallen into Allied hands. Iran has been defeated and ends up declaring war on Germany.

On *Shahrivar* 25 the radio announces that Reza Shah is abdicating in favor of his son, Mohammad Reza Pahlavi, who swears his oath on the Koran to the National Assembly and becomes Iran's new sovereign at the age of twenty-two.

The next day Iran is invaded jointly by the English and the Russians, and Reza Shah goes into exile with his entire family. They travel through Iran from north to south on the same road Talla and Sardar took but in the opposite direction. When they reach Bandar Abbas on the Persian Gulf they board an English ship bound for Mauritius. Reza Shah is never to return from exile, and dies in Johannesburg at the end of the war.

Iran is occupied but a spirit of freedom breathes through it on the wind. The new king distances himself from his father's policies, condemning his despotic behavior. He returns assets seized from the Uluma, frees political prisoners, promises to bring an end to mixed schools and to set up a department of theology at Tehran University. People flock back to Iran: the exiled, disgraced former friends or ministers of Reza Shah's, all those who escaped execution and who were forced or chose to move abroad or to Iran's far-flung provinces. Tribes dig up their buried weapons; their deposed leaders return from banishment and resume their titles—abolished ten years earlier by Reza Shah—as khan or sheik of their land. Mullahs reemerge from the libraries of their religious clubs, go back to their mosques, and start preaching again. Old politicians make a dignified return to the political scene, and young intellectuals eagerly publish books, newspapers, and manifestoes. Iran's thirteenth National Assembly comes together under foreign occupation. From now on the Assembly will appoint the prime minister, whose cabinet constantly falls and reinvents itself depending on the Shah's moods and his alliances with his deputies, the British, the Americans, and the Soviets.

The people of Iran have thrown off all the constraints imposed by Reza Shah, and many women now appear in public again in their chadors, while others choose to stop wearing the veil.

Talla, who has not worn one for years, follows her neighbors and friends in readopting the chador. She wears it out of propriety, without conviction, one with a pattern on a white background, the sort women used to wear only indoors. She ties it at her waist to free up her hands, and her hair can be seen sneaking out under the veil, her braids hang over her breasts and she makes no attempt to hide them. Never again will she wear a black chador or a *roubandeh*.

The new school year began a few days after the occupying soldiers arrived in Gholhak. When the headmaster stood before his war-befuddled pupils that morning at Djam School, he began his brief speech with the already famous words of Mohamma Ali Foroughi, the new prime minister, words he had spoken when his cabinet gave him a vote of confidence at the National Assembly: "They come and they shall go, for their own ends, and they have nothing against us."

Then the headmaster went on: "You should have no fear in your hearts, because Iran has been occupied by far more terrifying invaders than these, but life moves on and Iran still stands. You should be proud, my dear children, proud of your country. Don't go looking for fights, feel no hatred, this is not our war. Don't fret, they will leave. They're only here to pass through, and pass through they will, as all the others have . . . "

It was early in the fall and still hot enough for Bahram to be sleeping on the roof. With the curfews, the nights were even darker and the stars so low that you could sometimes see a whole veil of them shifting across the sky. On nights like these they said the imams traveled on the stars to attend receptions among them.

Up on the roof Bahram had no thoughts of war. He gazed at the sky and wondered how he could draw it. Whenever he had a pen in his hand he would draw, landscapes on pieces of paper, and fake tattoos on his arms, like those he noticed on the louts at the hammam. He drew with his left hand, his eyes unblinking. He lay on his back, stroking the gray and white kitten who slept with him, and who woke him at dawn by pawing playfully at his face. Despite her wariness of cats, Talla had given in to her son's pleading and the two of them were already inseparable, day and night. From where he lay he could hear people talking about the Germans, as people did all over town. And he wondered why the Germans had suddenly become the bad guys. He remembered the German women beside the pool with their white skin and golden hair. He thought of them as if the very thought were forbidden. A thought already forbidden because of the women's nakedness, but even more so now that the Germans were banished. So he thought it even more quietly, but he thought it all the same.

The Soviet soldiers who moved into Gholhak were Turks and Kazakhstanis. Wherever they were from, though, they would always be known as "the Russians." Even though they now called themselves "Soviets," there was still no mistaking them. The people here had known them too long to be fooled.

The Russian soldiers were hungry; they were given only black bread to eat. On the very day they arrived one of them stole food from a grocer and went into hiding. His troop set about searching for him and this added to the upheaval of having them in Gholhak. They were thirsty, too, and tramped through the streets pestering the inhabitants for water. Talla passed some over the wall to them. No one opened their doors; people had livestock and did not want this to be known. The Russians and English must not know anyone had livestock at home or they might come and take animals for slaughter; their soldiers were hungry.

Sometimes the soldiers also argued with the locals, who, once over their fear of foreigners, took no pity on these malnourished wretches. Of course religion encouraged everyone to help a neighbor in need, but no one even knew whether these were Muslims or infidels. Worse still, some said the Russians had lost their religion altogether, they had abandoned God, and God would abandon them. Talla could not really distinguish between Muslims and infidels, or between the pure and the impure. In a peasant woman's life, there was already

enough to do, so none would choose to add restrictive obligations. Talla had her own ways, like reciting a verse from the
Koran three times and blowing on an impure thing to make it
pure. She believed in these measures with all her might.

As soon as they arrived, the Russians installed a telegraph
line. The wires ran past Bahram's house and went all the way
to the Soviet embassy. For Bahram and his friends this was like
a new toy: They stole the wooden posts that held up the wires
and threw them into abandoned wells, leaving the wires to trail
on the ground and cutting off the communication. The
Russians were quick to repair the damage, and the children
sniggered. Before long, guards were put on duty to protect the
line. The children befriended the guards, who quickly grew
bored of standing by telegraph posts. They played together
with slingshots, and Bahram brought them water or milk and
occasionally even a cup of tea. Then the Allies withdrew from
the Tehran region, and the Russian soldiers left Gholhak.
Bahram pilfered some bread and cheese from Talla and gave
these provisions to a very young soldier called Omar who had
become his friend. It was meant for the journey but Omar ate
it all on the spot for fear of being robbed along the way.
Bahram went back home and brought him a bowl of dried fruit
to put in his pockets, and he gave him a piece of paper with his
name written on it so Omar could write him letters and send
him news. Then, copying Talla's routine, Bahram recited a
surah from the Koran and blew on the soldier to protect him
from evil. Omar did not understand what his friend expected
of him and all he saw in the Persian writing on that piece of
paper was a souvenir drawing.

B ahram would see blond women again, in a film this time. They were the same, exactly the same, but American. So were German women not the only ones with blond hair? Bahram had believed for a while that the Allies did not like the Germans because their women were debauched, and too beautiful. That couldn't have been it, though . . .

But the first time Bahram went to a movie screening there were no blond women in the film. In their barracks the Russian soldiers had set up a mobile projector and a white curtain on which they showed anti-Nazi propaganda films. During the projection one of the Russians gave a commentary in Turkish, and someone did his best to translate. No one was interested in the subject; they were all fascinated by the machine.

Talla attended that first screening. Talla and movies! Movies would never wonder what a woman like Talla might understand of them, but Talla would do a lot of thinking about movies. How could human beings possibly walk on a curtain? And now there were others coming up behind them, and vehicles too, where on earth had they come from when the only thing behind the curtain was its lining? And why didn't it all overflow, why didn't the marching soldiers fall on the floor in front of the curtain? And all these things seemed to exist in a real world, trees, buildings, the ground, the sky, all of it! Even war. And it was all nothing. Nothing that matched Talla's understanding of a real world. It was enough to drive her crazy!

Who could explain the movies to Talla? No one. And Talla never did understand what movies were, nor television when it arrived. Although television, which came to Iran in the late 1950s, seemed more plausible to her, because of the set itself, which could house this miniature population. This was a perfectly acceptable hypothesis for someone who had believed all her life in enchanted creatures of every shape and size. She spoke to the characters on the screen, saying hello and wishing them goodnight. Now elderly and believing she was being watched, she made sure the room was tidy and she was sitting nicely before turning on the set. Sometimes the people on the screen irritated her and she threw insults at them, but the rest of the time she was very friendly.

It was when he was nine that Bahram had an opportunity to go to a real movie theater. Mohsen, his friend Ali-Agha's older brother, took them to Tehran's Lalehzar Street, which Naser al-Din Shah had had built like the Champs Elysées after a trip to Paris: a street full of theaters and cinemas where black-and-white movies from the Western world were screened with Persian subtitles—detective movies, action movies, love stories, and westerns. Which is why, with apologies to Naser al-Din Shah, some called it Texas Street!

It was Mohsen's first time, too, and he made a mistake, taking them to a theater where no one asked to see their tickets. Slightly surprised, they thought they had had a good deal, and sat themselves down. Other people came and sat down, the room filled up, and then a man came and made a speech: They realized the room had been booked by a private school. Children dressed as angels and demons came on stage and put on what the three boys thought was a very strange show. They headed back to Gholhak confused and disappointed but on their way home, Bahram remembered something that had happened that morning. Just before he set off to the movies he had seen a hen that had been missing for over a month coming up from the bottom of the yard. Behind her was a chick, then another, then a third; in all nine chicks appeared out of nowhere. Bahram had squealed so loudly that Talla was startled. At the sight of these abundant gifts from God, she smothered her son with kisses and gave him an extra coin to buy some candy. Now Bahram cursed the hen, which, by arriving with such pomp, had monopolized all of the day's good luck so there was nothing but bad luck left for the hours to come.

They soon went back to Lalehzar Street. This time they bought three tickets and went into a proper movie theater with a royal box, which stayed empty that day. They watched a gangster film and Bahram sat openmouthed through the whole screening. Men in suits and hats with revolvers in their pockets strolled about with beautiful blond women; they killed other men who stepped out of fabulous cars, with other blond women in clinging, full-length dresses, women who wore dazzling jewels and dead foxes around their necks. Back at home, Bahram and Ali-Agha started playing gangsters; they roamed Gholhak's vacant lots pretending to sneer at revolvers, step out of cars, escort beautiful women . . .

That film fueled their games for several years, until they were about fifteen and old enough to go back to the movies on their own. Movies soon became their passion, as it was for all the capital's inhabitants, and the city's movie theaters were always full.

Talla, the mistrustful peasant woman who had not known any sort of refinement, still never neglected Norouz, the Zoroastrian New Year and one of its major feast days. It fell on the spring equinox, in the first month of the zodiacal calendar.

In preparation for the coming year, the last few weeks of winter were spent in spring cleaning. Talla completely emptied out both rooms in her house, the one on the ground floor and the one above it. She thoroughly washed everything that could be washed: curtains, bedcovers, carpets, etc. She cleaned the rooms from top to bottom and then put everything back where it belonged. In other homes this process was an opportunity to throw out anything that was in the way or of no use. But Talla never threw anything away, not even scraps of wood or bits of string found in the street. The more she hoarded around her, the more reassuring she found it. When she ran out of room, she consented to move things to the shed Sardar had built in the yard so that he did not have live alongside the bricks and metal rods Talla picked up in the street.

When the house was clean and tidy, she tackled the hen-house and the stable, and finished with the yard and its pond.

After this, because tradition required every family to wear new clothes for the changing of the year, they would go together to choose them. There was no debate about Bahram's outfit; they went to the tailor and ordered a suit just the right size, or perhaps a little bigger so he could wear it all year, and they had a couple of white shirts made for him. The tailor also sold underwear and socks. Then they went to the cobbler and bought a pair of thick leather slip-on shoes. Talla had a neighbor make her a long dress and a pair of leggings in cheap fabric. Sardar never bought himself an entirely new outfit. He might replace some pants, a shirt, very occasionally a jacket. Some years he would make do with a new pair of socks. Sardar did not go to Bahram's tailor, but to the old sewing man who could not make fashionable suits and supplied him with pants held at the waist with string. Farangi pants were not for him. But for Bahram, yes. His son was an extension of him, his continuity; himself but better, his reflection in the modern world. So then, let Bahram wear smart clothes, let him go to school, to the movies . . .

On New Year's Day they put on their new clothes and sat in their family room at a table covered with a cloth on which Talla had prepared *Haft Sin*. This comprised seven elements all of which had names beginning with S, and symbolized wishes for the year to come: *Sabzeh*, grains of wheat, for rebirth; *Samanu*, wheat dough, for abundance; *Senjed*, dried jujube fruit, for love; *Sib*, apples, for beauty and good health; *Sonbol*, hyacinth flowers, for the onset of spring; *Serkeh*, vinegar, for age and patience; and a few *Sekkeh*, coins, for prosperity. Other things Talla had put on the table were a mirror, the one from her wedding day; a bowl containing an orange, which, in ancient times, apparently represented the earth hovering in space; a vial of rosewater from her village; and lastly the Koran. In those days she did not include goldfish or colored eggs.

Now they waited till they heard the cannon fire announcing the changing of the year at the exact moment when the sun passed over the equator. They never missed this moment, even if it happened in the middle of the night. Talla recited prayers and when the cannon boomed they all kissed each other. Then she would take from the Koran a bill she had slipped between the pages. She handed it to Bahram, who had been tempted a hundred times to open the Koran and see how big a bill it was.

They ate fish for the first meal of the new year, the only time in the year that they did. Talla bought it in the market, smoked fish from the Caspian Sea in the north, and she reheated it in rice seasoned with herbs.

Sardar was particularly happy because during the festivities radio programming was different, with radio plays, more music, and a jaunty note in the announcers' voices. And Bahram was happy, too, because it was the only school holiday except for the summer vacation, and he would get a bit of money and could eat a lot of sweet foods.

Next came all the visiting, in descending age order. First people visited family, starting with the oldest members, then friends, then neighbors. After this, everyone who had been visited would come back to visit them in the same order, but it inevitably grew very disorderly. Passersby in the streets wore their best clothes. Women went out without chadors, their faces powdered, their lips outlined and perfectly colored, and with bows in their hair. Those in chadors wore them over new shoes. Men had slicked-back hair, and children proudly wore their new clothes. Tables were laden with pastries and sweet treats for Norouz. Children were repeatedly told not to help themselves until there were guests in the house, that they mustn't take too much "because that's rude and brings shame on us." Talla bought special Norouz cakes, too, and hid them far from Bahram's grasping fingers. The Amirs had no family in Tehran or in Shemiran; their visits were restricted to neighbors, local people, and a few dignitaries who had to be wished a happy new year but who would not come to visit them.

Adults would usually give children gifts of money at Norouz, but there were so many children in the neighborhood that it would have meant ruination to give a bill to each of them. So the only other bill Bahram could be sure of receiving

was from Mahtab-Khanoum, their immediate neighbor and
Talla's oldest friend. The dignitaries would also sometimes give
him money, but the exact amount could vary considerably
depending on their mood.

The New Year celebrations and school holidays lasted thirteen days, because the ancient Persians believed that each of
the twelve signs of the zodiac would reign over the earth for a
thousand years and then would come the thirteenth era, the
era of chaos.

D espite the occupation, Norouz 1322 is celebrated with joy. Then, almost before the spring has started, the campaign for the legislative elections of the fourteenth Iranian parliament begins. It is the fiercest fight there has ever been on the country's political scene. The monarchists, democrats, socialists, communists, liberals, and religious adherents—all of whom might or might not be pro-Soviet, pro-English, or pro-American—fight to win seats for their representatives and loyal followers. And for the first time Gholhak's workers take an interest in the electoral campaign.

Sardar walks over Gholhak's hills and gazes into the distance. Here he hears only pleasant things: silence barely disturbed by the tinkle of bells from a flock of sheep that a shepherd is grazing on the opposite hillside. At forty-three Sardar has the authenticity of an unbowed spirit, a man who has created for himself a world in keeping with his own wishes. He is tall and thin with broad shoulders, dark skin, black eyes, low eyebrows, and a piercing, noble expression. A short, graying beard covers half of his sculpted face lined with deep wrinkles that have nothing to do with old age but are a mark of durability. His hair is still black, his back still upright, and his bearing always aloof. He looks at the mountain, its snow-capped, conical majesty. He likes looking at his mountains. As he walks he hums a tune from Ghamsar, a song about mountains, in fact. He has often wondered what might lie beyond these mountains, but he can feel age catching up with him, he no

longer has the strength to go see for himself. He feels that had
he been born here, he would definitely have made the journey;
he would not have tolerated not knowing. He thinks there is a
desert on the far side of these mountains, and beyond that
more mountains. He has been told that beyond them is the sea.
But he does not believe this. People have such strange ideas.
One day his son will go to see and confirm this for him, show
him photos. Sardar will shake his head, grind his teeth, and say
a disappointed "Allahu Akbar," now knowing there is nothing
but a chain of mountains between him and the edge of the
earth.

Sardar walks over the hillside, brushing pebbles aside with
his stick. Then he stops, takes off his headdress, squats down
on the ground, and takes a deep breath of Shemiran's fine,
pure air. He has reached his decision: he will not vote this time,
either. His neighbor Mirza has told him he must vote. Mirza
has a son who has learned to read: His eldest son Mohsen has
had adult literacy lessons. He reads the papers laboriously but
conscientiously, so he now knows about politics and tells his
father whom he should vote for. And he really should vote.
Sardar will not go, he is happy to be illiterate, not putting his
nose in any of those people's affairs. What if he made the
wrong choice? Who knows who these men really are? "I'm just
a shepherd, a smallholder, I deal with livestock and land, not
men." He therefore agrees with Mossadegh's intention to with-
draw the right to vote from illiterate individuals who will simply vote for whomever their feudal lord, their khan or sheik,
tells them to. Sardar knows this for himself, he does not need
Mossadegh to tell him, he does not want to be anyone else's
sheep. Sardar acts only when no other man stands between
him and the job to be done.

At the end of 1322, the fourteenth Iranian National Assembly
comes together, comprising twenty-six deputies and seven par-
liamentary groups. They are all there, even the communists

have secured a seat. They have come from every corner of Iran, from the south occupied by the English, the north occupied by the USSR, the unoccupied zones, from every ethnicity, tribe, and language. Most of them are rich, titled, or at least from important families, and with diplomas from European universities. They have all come and are about to start their sessions of endless debating and shouting in the Assembly building. For now, as they stride like conquerors marching triumphantly to the temple, they are convinced they will perform miracles for the Iran of tomorrow. And Sardar has no part in it, and Talla does not even count.

I n these uncertain times, the Amir family wants for noth-ing. Sardar watches over his livestock and tends the land he now owns; with the passing years he has steadily bought up more plots, and together they are beginning to con-stitute a handsome property. They have their own meat, fruit, and vegetables, and there is plenty of water.

Talla cooks in earthenware pots on a wood-fire oven dug into the ground. She makes her own bread, too. She spreads the dough on a round mat of thick fabric then sticks the loaf to the side of the oven. Once it is cooked, the bread falls away from the side and onto the grate, and then it can be removed with a wooden paddle. Talla herself takes it out with her bare hands, her toughened skin can tolerate the heat. Sometimes she makes *toutak*, sugary biscuits with almonds or walnuts, and if she adds milk to them she can make *nan-e shirmal*. She also knows how to make a different sort of bread cooked on top of the oven, known as nomad's bread.

Bahram's friends like coming to his house because they are always allowed to fill their stomachs with Sardar's watermel-ons, to dip their fingers in Talla's pots of cream and yogurt, or to eat their fill of dried fruit, *toutak*, or *nan-e shirmal*. On top of this, as an only child, Bahram has more pocket money than his friends from large families, always enough to buy a rial or two of candy from a peddler and share it with them. In the spring they paddle in Gholhak's unnamed river. In summer they go to the swimming pool in Davoudieh or find a body of water near Gholhak where they can swim. And they always end up in the shade of the old trees in the Amirs' garden while Talla climbs to the top of the mulberry tree and shakes it to make the fruit drop, and the boys gather it up and eat it with childish glee.

And to the pleasures of moments like that, another delight is gradually added: girls and their perfume. Bahram has started looking at them shyly, and has noticed the beautiful Saname, a girl his own age who goes to Gholhak's girls' school. For some time now Bahram has stopped racing home at the end of the school day, but slows his pace in order to walk behind Saname. He watches her from behind. She has a long, neatly plaited braid that falls to her waist and is embellished with an impeccably tied ribbon. Her gray uniform is perfectly ironed, her shoes meticulously polished, and her ankle socks with their silky edging always immaculately white. This girl is cared for. Every morning a loving hand combs her long black hair, plaits her braid, and carefully ties the white ribbon, never the previous day's ribbon, but a new, clean, ironed one, then her clothes are checked over, she is given a kiss and sent off to school. Saname is the daughter of the man who owns the Iran Cement factory. Bahram, who has dreamed of nothing but blond hair and white skin since seeing the German women, falls under the spell of this dark-haired, dusky-skinned girl. Dark as night and delicate as dawn.

On Fridays, Bahram and his friends play soccer on a pitch close to Saname's house, near her father's factory. They have only a bundle of rags tied together for a ball, and it is too light, which means they have to kick it very hard, sending pebbles flying through the air along with the ball. If he sees her on these Fridays she wears pretty colorful dresses and carries a purse like a lady.

Bahram ends up passionately in love, and when he arrives home from soccer one day he begs his mother to go and ask for

Saname's hand on his behalf. To which Talla replies: "Hush now, you're only ten." His age means nothing, Bahram wants her. So he decides to go see Mash-Hakim, who makes amulets and magic potions, to ask him for an elixir of love. "Bring me three tomans, and I'll give it to you," says Mash-Hakim.

Bahram cannot think how to come by three tomans. He has only one. "Could you give me two tomans?" he asks his mother. "I need them."

"Don't even think it," she replies.

Bahram waits a few days, then renews his attack, saying it is for a soccer ball, then for school, all the pupils are being asked for two tomans, then he offers to work for his mother two Fridays running to earn two tomans. Talla thinks this is far too much to pay. In the end she gives in without asking anything in exchange. Bahram takes the three tomans to the old talisman maker who mixes up various solid and liquid ingredients and hands him a vial of a blackish oily substance.

"Pour this in water and give it to her to drink," he says.

"If I could get her to drink something I wouldn't need you."

"Ah well, you didn't tell me that. In that case it's more expensive. You need to give me another five tomans."

Five tomans! Bahram cannot ask Talla for more money so he decides to sell his postcard collection—his forty-three post-cards from all over the world, things he cherishes more than his pigeons. He parts with them sadly and gets four tomans for them. And he steals one toman from Talla, he has no choice. Talla thinks she has lost it and curses for days. Bahram gives the money to Mash-Hakim and receives a different vial in return.

"Pour this in water and throw the water in front of her so she walks on it . . . "

After school the next day, Bahram races home, fills a bucket of water, and runs over to Saname's house to wait for her. As soon as he sees her he pours the contents of the vial into the bucket and when Saname is only yards away he empties the bucket over the sidewalk. He waits to check that she steps into the love potion and then runs away.

That very evening Bahram tells his parents he is going to sleep in the garden. He makes his bed close to the garden door and waits till his mother locks it for the night. Once his parents are asleep he gets up quietly, unlocks the door, and leaves it ajar. Then he lies down and waits for the bewitched Saname to join him on his bed.

But she did not come, not that evening, nor the next, nor on any other night.

He went back to Mash-Hakim in despair, but the potion maker reassured him: "She will absolutely definitely come. Wait a little longer." Bahram was patient and opened the garden door ever wider when he heard footsteps ringing in the still of the night, hoping they were Saname's . . .

In the fall, Bahram packed away his love for Saname as a lost cause, and sought comfort in drawing. He drew a lot and with increasing skill. Some of his pictures were hung on the classroom wall; the headmaster even chose one for his office. As an excellent sprinter, Bahram was the star of the school's athletics team. And he was conspicuous for his very good grades in history and geography. The headmaster of Djam started taking an interest in him: "If out of a hundred pupils we can produce one elite individual for the nation, we have fulfilled our duty," he confided to his wife, also a teacher. And in Bahram he had found this longed-for elite individual.

He instigated a discreet, methodically planned strategy. He took to summoning Bahram to his office from time to time, and this disconcerted the boy, who had no idea of the headmaster's plans. On each occasion the man wore a serious expression and would ask Bahram to stand and wait by his desk, then in a clipped voice he would issue an order which Bahram interpreted as a punishment: "You'll stay behind after school today and write out the schedule for the athletics team" or "This evening you can draw me a landscape to hang in . . . " Then, when the time came and because the headmaster knew Bahram had an interest in history, he asked the boy to read particular newspapers and cut out the most interesting articles about international events and bring them to him once a month.

Bahram was not yet eleven when he handed his first set of

articles to the headmaster; the subject was the Tehran confer-
ence. All the papers used the same photo: Churchill,
Roosevelt, and Stalin sitting in different-sized chairs on the terrace of the Soviet embassy. Roosevelt's chair was higher than
the other two, and Churchill was more sprawled in a wider,
lower armchair. He looked apprehensive, had put his military
cap on his left knee, and was looking down. Roosevelt had
crossed his legs and appeared thoughtful. Stalin, on the other
hand, seemed buoyant and looked straight at the lens. They
had come all that way to settle a number of issues: the arrangements for the Normandy landings, the Polish border, the
future of Yugoslavia . . . Bahram had read it all, concentrating
and motivated. The headmaster accepted this roundup of
press coverage with interest and asked him to summarize it
orally. Bahram did as he was asked, naming the key figures,
their position and nationality, outlining the terms of their
alliance, and citing the enemies they had in common. The
headmaster added that they had promised Iran territorial
integrity, the withdrawal of their troops at the end of the war,
and compensation for the occupation . . . and then he congratulated Bahram. It was very likely thanks to this modest
exercise that Bahram found his vocation and became an expert
on World War II. He would learn its every detail, every place
and date, the most minor anecdote. He would come back to it
all through his life, in every conversation, with didactic accu-
racy and a formidable command of the Persian language. He
also identified where he personally came in the chronology of
the Second World War, and whenever he was asked for his
date of birth, 1933, he would always point out it was the year
Hitler came to power in Germany.

It is about 7:30 on the morning of *Khordad* 2nd, 1325. Bahram is walking in the shade of trees along Telephone-khaneh Street. On the left are a few houses hidden behind their walls, Mash-Rahim's grocery shop, and the telephone exchange. To the right there is just a row of trees and a dusty stretch of wasteland. When he is level with the grocer's shop he spots the zinc roof of a huge house far away in the distance through the trees. This is the summer residence of a Tehrani nobleman, a general in the army; in summer, high-ranking families escape the heat of the city and take refuge in Shemiran, making the most of the cool mountain air. Thanks to their cars, the men frequently travel back and forth to Tehran, but the women and children stay here for the whole summer, enjoying their sheltered gardens. The gates open, cars come and go, the passengers' hats can be seen, and occasionally one of them turns around and looks toward you, or even into your eyes, even the women. Those women look you in the eye and all you can do is look away. How could anyone look into the eyes of these women who are too beautiful and too heavily made-up to be real? Sometimes when Bahram walks along the walls to their properties he hears laughter, a cry, or even music: a garden party. Everyone uses the English words "garden party," even the servants, the maids and the gardener say it: "They're having a garden party tonight." And now the locals have taken to saying, "They're having a garden party," if their neighbors make noise. The sound of those foreign words in Talla's mouth when she refers to her hens cackling in her own yard somehow rings true although she does not even realize she is speaking English. Much later an outrageous rumor would circulate around Gholhak about a certain young lady from that residence: The general's daughter was in love with Bahram. The maid entrusted with delivering the note would give the secret away, and this would be the final touch, establishing Bahram definitively as Gholhak's hero, the boy who triumphed over the indifference of the nobility.

But at the moment they have not reached that point, they will have to wait until the end of the month of *Khordad* and the beginning of the school summer vacation when their cars will arrive one behind the other and everyone will remember that, come what may, they return every year.

When he reaches Shermiran Road, which climbs straight up toward the mountain, Bahram can feel the cooler wind caressing his shaven head and sneaking inside his white shirt, which starts to flutter. Bahram has six white shirts, one for each school day. Two are from last year and are too small; another two are too big and he has to roll up their sleeves. The remaining two are the right size, and he is wearing one of these today. Good peasant that she is, Talla does no ironing; in fact, she does not even have an iron. Once she has washed the shirts, she pulls them in every direction before laying them out flat, and they end up looking pretty good. Bahram changes his shirt every day like boys from good families. His mother adds a touch of powdered lapis lazuli to the washing water, giving it a pronounced azure color, and a vague echo of this blue is left on his white shirts after they have been rinsed.

His pants, on the other hand, are too short, only reaching his ankles, and they have been mended a dozen times. But the worst of it are his shoes—they are so tight that he never has a chance to stop thinking about them. In this dusty terrain, the only thing that counts is an immaculate white shirt.

For a moment Bahram closes his eyes and savors the gentle breeze. He has a lot on his mind. He is about to finish sixth grade, the last year of primary school. At the start of the next academic year, he will be in high school, but there is no high school in Gholhak. He either has to stop his schooling or head north to Tadjrish or south to Tehran.

Bahram does not intend to stop his studies, but how will this work? His family has no car and no horse-drawn cart. The nearest school is in Tadjrish, in the foothills of the mountains. It would be almost impossible to travel that far on foot twice a day, perhaps even four times if he includes the lunch break. And then he needs to think about the winter, which is harsh in Shemiran, the snow and the cold. There is a bus to Tadjrish, but you can never tell what time it will come through town. In spite of all this, Bahram would do it, he would get up early and make do with no lunch, but the problem is Talla. She has decreed that she will not let her only son go so far away, even if this means he must stop attending school. Meanwhile Sardar wants only one thing, for his son to do everything he himself has not done in life, everything he did not want to do. Sardar, who has always chosen to stand apart from the crowd, who never believed in the advantages of moving up the social scale, is well aware he must not impose these ideas of his on his son. Bahram is from here; whatever happens he must not be a peasant all his life. In Ghamsar everyone was the same; even though Sardar was from one of the more influential families, the discrepancy was not particularly striking. But here the parameters are different and he knows that if his son does not change his social standing he will suffer for it. But Sardar's concept of society is not sufficiently developed for him to grasp the difference between graduating school after sixth grade and going further. He feels that what Bahram has achieved in school so far is already quite something and if the boy stopped now it would do nothing to hamper his own ambitions for his son.

Bahram crosses Shermiran Road and turns into Deh Street. He stops outside the school, closes his eyes again, and briefly savors the soft feeling of the wind once more. When he opens his eyes, he sees the plaque with the big, bold words "Djam School," and he suddenly has a brilliant idea: "Oh my, why did no one think of this before!"

Over the last month he and Ghassem and Siavosh have been knocking on doors to find a solution; they have talked to Gholhak's dignitaries to get them to open a seventh grade class at the school. They even went to see the wife of Amidi-e Nouri, the big newspaper director. She is a charitable woman, happy to speak to anyone, and she listened to them kindly. But she told them she could not open all the doors. In fact, no one has succeeded in opening this particular door.

Bahram cannot see Ghassem in the schoolyard.

"I have to find him, I have to find him, the bell is about to go . . ."

They have done their research, found names and addresses, and introduced themselves in wealthier households. Sometimes they were turned away on the spot by the caretaker; other times they were shown in and they managed to say a few words to the master. To no effect. And yet it was Reza Shah who encouraged their love for their country, their duty to their nation which they would perform through knowledge. It was Reza Shah who wanted to educate an elite, so surely he could not encourage them to dream one minute and summarily abandon them the next.

Bahram sees Ghassem at last and runs over to him.

"I've got it, I've got it: We're going to go and see Djam himself, the man the school is named after. He'll give us our new class. We'll go see him this evening. He lives somewhere around here."

The bell rings and the students stand in lines. The headmaster comes out of the building and inspects his pupils. As he does every morning, he walks with his hands behind his back, scrutinizing each child. He knows every pupil's first name but always uses their family name, and he always shouts: "Hosseini, take your hands out of your pockets," or, "Akbarzadeh, why do you look like a street beggar?"

The children instantly stand to attention, backs stiff, chins held high, with their eyes on the horizon, their arms by their sides, and the palms of their hands pressed to their thighs. This fifteen minutes every morning is a nightmare for them: Anyone who dares utter a word or step out of line provokes the headmaster's anger and risks *falak*. When the inspection is over the children sing the national anthem then chant, "Long live our country, long live the Shah!" and they can at last go to their classrooms.

At noon Bahram goes home for lunch. Talla is sitting waiting for him in the garden. Sardar does not come home in the middle of the day; he takes bread, cheese, and some fruit when he sets off in the morning. Talla has already spread the cloth on the ground in the garden, and has laid out two plates, two spoons, two glasses, and some bread. And a pan is simmering on the fire.

As soon as Bahram arrives she gets up to draw water from the well and hands a glass to Bahram, who downs the cold water in one. This well water is incredibly cold even though it is forty degrees outside.

Talla serves him meat and carrots with a tomato sauce. Bahram eats it with a soft thin flatbread that his mother collects every day before the call to prayer at noon so that it is fresh for lunch. Sitting cross-legged on the ground, Bahram eats as fast as he can. When he has had enough his mother makes him some tea. He wishes he could have a nap but it would make him late for school. He spends another two hours at school in the afternoon, then comes home for his nap under the mulberry tree, in the coolest spot in the garden.

Bahram is woken by his father's footsteps—is it that late? He jumps out of bed.

"I have to go."

"Go where?" Sardar asks.

"To see Djam for the new class."

"Djam!"

"Yes, Djam. The school's named after him, isn't it, so he'll definitely do something."

"Do you know who Djam is? He's Minister of Court!"

Djam was indeed Minister of Court, among other things. But before that, in the Qajar era, Mahmud Djam, who learned French at a Jesuit school, had been a translator in Tabriz. He came to Tehran and started working at the Ministry of Finance, gradually climbing through the hierarchy and taking on different jobs until he ended up at the top of the pyramid and became Reza Shah's prime minister in 1314. He was Prime Minister when the veil was banned. He resigned that position in 1318 and became Minister of Court. After Reza Shah left he was appointed as the Iranian ambassador to Egypt, and later became a minister again, then an ambassador, then a senator . . .

Sardar does not know exactly what position Djam currently holds, but "Minister of Court" is the title he remembers. Like all Gholhakis, he knows little about power, but knows something about the members of parliament who have properties in Gholhak. And Djam is a prince among princes, the highest-ranking of Gholhak's dignitaries. And the only thing any of the locals remember about him is that he is Minister of Court, because in their view this is the most fascinating position of all those in power. Sometimes he seems still more mysterious than the Shah himself because he needs to know not only all of the Shah's secrets but plenty of other secrets to which the Shah is not privy.

And Bahram wants to go and see Djam! Sardar will have to put him off the idea because, without a shadow of a doubt, he would be greeted with nothing but crushing humiliation if he went to knock on such an elevated door.

"He doesn't have time for peasants like us."

"If that's true, then why's the school named after him?"

"He may not have asked for it to be. Maybe it was called Djam because he had a house here. They won't even let you through the door."

"Well, we're going and we'll see what happens."

"Do you at least know how to address a minister? You have to say . . . " Sardar has forgotten, or never knew, gets confused between the king and a minister. "You say: Your most distinguished Majesty, the honorable Minister Djam."

Bahram puts on his shoes, but his mother asks him to wait. She goes over to the well and hauls up the pail of fruit, chooses a peach and four apricots, wraps them in a piece of cloth, and hands them to him, telling him to eat them on the way. Bahram takes the fruit in one hand and a pitcher of water in the other. He gulps it down so quickly that the water runs out of his mouth, down his neck, and all the way to his navel, then he empties the rest over his head and sets off at a run. At the end of the unnamed pathway, Bahram turns around and comes back home, he's forgotten his jacket: You can't visit a minister without a jacket. Talla forgot to recite a surah from the Koran and to blow on his face, so she keeps him back a moment longer.

On Thursdays school ends at lunchtime. Back home, Talla has already spread out the tablecloth. Today she has made bread herself, delicious little rolls that are crusty on top and doughy in the middle. Sardar will be happy: "It's like bread from the village." Bahram wolfs his food down and then lies on the ground next to the cloth.

"I mustn't go to sleep. If I fall asleep, wake me up when you've finished doing the dishes."

Talla fills a bowl with water from the pond, wets the plates and glasses, scrubs them with a handful of dirt from the yard, then rinses everything out. The pond water is murky, not safe to drink, and she uses it only for washing. She rinses the tableware a second time with fresh well water. Then she wraps the remaining bread in a big napkin, winding it around several times, otherwise the heat and the dry air will turn it hard before the evening.

She waits a few minutes before saying, "Bahram *jan*, Bahram *jan*, get up, my son." He is fast asleep. "Bahram *jan*, Bahram *agha* . . . " He does not react. She leaves him to sleep and lies down beside him under the mulberry tree. She is tired but must not fall asleep, she needs to wake Bahram. In the meantime she turns toward him and studies him in profile. Then she puts her arm around his head and hugs him to her. Bahram's head is buried between her breasts and this wakes him. He leaps to his feet and curses at Talla, then hurries upstairs and comes straight back down with his jacket on. His mother follows him to the door, reciting a surah from the Koran and blowing on his face.

Bahram runs over to Telephone-khaneh Street, and waits for Ghassem under the old plane tree. It is forty degrees in the shade and Bahram sweats in his wool jacket. It is siesta time, and there is not a soul to be seen. They have to go to Djam's house at four o'clock, they have been granted an audience. Bahram does not have a watch, but there is bound to be someone to tell them the time.

Ghassem strolls up to him nonchalantly.

"Where the hell have you been? What if it's already four?"

"But four o'clock must be later than siesta time."

"Okay, well, let's go. We need to get Siavosh," Bahram says, setting off at a run.

"Bahram!" Ghassem cries. "It's too hot to run."

Bahram slows to a walk and picks up pebbles, which he aims at the trunks of trees on the other side of the street.

Sweat beads on their shaven heads, running over their foreheads and dripping from their eyelashes. Bahram wipes it away with the sleeve of his jacket. Ghassem is not wearing a jacket; the one from his school uniform has been patched too many times to be worn in front of Djam, so he is wearing the smart shirt he and his older brother share for important occasions. It is a little too big for him. There are seven children in his family: four boys and three girls. The two older girls are already married, the third is engaged to a cousin and is waiting until she is sixteen to be married. Of the four boys, Ghassem is second in age. His father used to be a coachman, he drove a horse-drawn cart taking goods to Shemiran: bricks, wood, rice . . . The horse and cart were his own. As he himself admitted, he treated his horses better than his own children. But competition from cars ruined his business, and he now works at the Iran Cement factory to the west of Gholhak. He is a cheerful man with no regrets. Times change and so does he.

Ghassem's mother is pregnant with her eighth child and his father is happy, every child is a gift. Next year he will get work for his eldest son at the factory with him. The boy is among the first cohort to go through Djam School, just like Ghassem, they are in the same class. Their father is proud of his sons; they have learned to read. The older boy will finish school this year, after graduating sixth grade, and will work at the factory like his father. Eldest sons take the same job as their fathers; the others have to find something for themselves. Ghassem's father believes in education. He is delighted to see his son dashing around trying to secure another class for his school, even though deep down he does not really believe it will happen. That does not stop him having the wildest dreams of one day seeing his son become a civil servant. He need only graduate ninth grade . . . so he lets him go along with Bahram on this adventure. You never know!

Siavosh joins them. He is the son of a local administrator; his father works at Gholhak's town council. He is from an educated family from Kerman. His grandfather was a mullah and a supporter of the constitutional revolution. They are one of Gholhak's respectable families, but they have no wealth. If a seventh grade class is not established in Gholhak, his father will send him to high school whatever the cost. Their family ambition dictates that Siavosh should go on to higher education. And anyway, his father has no intention of festering in Gholhak's council offices; he is waiting for an opening at the ministry.

What time is it? None of the passersby they meet has a watch.

Bahram has an idea.

"Let's go to the police station," he says and runs off.

But Ghassem is thirsty and says, "We're going to the mosque first for a drink."

There is a blind man sitting by a bucket of water in the

courtyard of Gholhak's mosque. They ask him for some water and the blind man says, "Drink and pray."

They each drink a ladleful of water and set off again.

"Pray," Ghassem reminds them. And pray they do.

There is no one outside the police station. Two uniformed officers in peaked caps are sweltering in the shade of the inner courtyard.

"What time is it please, *Agha*?"

"It's siesta time!"

"The actual time, please, two o'clock, three?" he pleads.

"Why do you want to know the time, little man?"

"We have an appointment."

"An appointment?" the policeman laughs.

"Please." Bahram is close to tears.

"I don't have a watch. Go ask in the office."

Bahram runs over and finds a policeman sitting at a desk. His hat is not on his head but on the desk.

"Salam, *Agha*."

"Yes?"

"Do you know what time it is, please?"

"Have you come to the police station to know the time?"

"The men outside told me to come ask you."

Siavosh has followed Bahram into the office, and now joins in: "Good afternoon, lieutenant. Please could you tell us the time?"

The policeman gives a self-important smile. He is flattered: He is not a lieutenant, just an under officer. He stands up, takes his watch from the pocket of his pants, and flips it open.

"It's three twenty-five."

"Thank you, *Agha*," says Bahram.

"Thank you, lieutenant!" says Siavosh.

"Thank you, lieutenant!" Bahram repeats.

Bahram comes out of the office and throws a "thank you, *Agha* lieutenants!" at the policemen, then he takes Ghassem's arm and starts running again.

"So what time is it?" asks one of the policemen.

"Three twenty-five," Bahram cries, already far away.

"Stop running," Ghassem complains. "What's three twenty-five compared to four o'clock?"

"It's earlier."

"Yes, but how much earlier? Earlier earlier or just earlier?"

"I don't know but we're going now."

At the entrance to the grounds Bahram strikes the knocker three times.

"Coming, coming," the caretaker replies straightaway as if he has been waiting for them.

"Salam, *Agha.*"

"Salam, boys, come in."

A magnificent, extensive garden like a rose garden fit for a prince. The house is not visible at first but appears at a turn in the driveway, appropriately elegant with its two upper floors and its balconies and balustrades draped with jasmine. The caretaker takes them onto a path that cuts across to the back door of the house. They go down five steps and enter a remarkably cool room with a vaulted ceiling. An old man sits cross-legged on a worn carpet, with his back against the wall. Bahram thinks this old man was probably meant to open the door.

"Give these kids a cordial," the caretaker tells the old man. "They're going to see *Agha.* They're thirsty, poor boys."

The old man leans on his stick to haul himself to his feet then disappears behind a curtain. The boys stand in the middle of the empty room, heads lowered, eyes on the floor. The old man comes back using only one hand to carry a tray with four glasses on it. The caretaker takes the tray and hands it to the boys. Bahram takes a glass—it's full of cherry cordial and ice cubes! It is so big he has to hold it with both hands. The boys' eyes are popping out of their heads. There is an ice

salesman on Shermiran Road; they sometimes see him breaking big blocks of ice, but only the rich buy it. They gulp down
the cordial greedily.

"Easy, easy, you'll spill it on your clothes," says the caretaker, who has already drained his own glass. There are only ice
cubes left in it; he picks one out, rubs it on his forehead and
cheeks, then pops it in his mouth. He looks at the boys as if
inviting them to do the same. Bahram copies him, but having
the ice cube in his mouth gives him a headache. He takes it out,
holds it in his hand, and watches it melt. The caretaker
crunches his ice cube and it makes a noise as it breaks between
his teeth. Bahram and Ghassem put theirs back into their
mouth and crunch them too—Bahram has a headache again.
The caretaker takes a handkerchief from his pocket, wipes his
face and hands, then wipes the boys' hands.

"Wait here, I'm going to see if *Agha* can see you now."

The old man says nothing, he has not said a word since they
arrived; he is sitting cross-legged with his back to the wall
again, as if waiting to die.

The caretaker returns and asks the boys to follow him. They
climb back up the five steps, come out of the house and onto
the main drive. They think they will be going into the house
through the main entrance but the caretaker takes a different
path that leads to the garden.

Djam is here playing with a small dog, a breed Bahram has
never seen before.

"These are the boys I told you about, sir," the caretaker
says.

Djam turns toward them.

"Go on," says the caretaker, and he leaves.

They have all agreed: Bahram will do the talking. Bahram
takes three steps forward. Djam is wearing a sort of garnet colored robe in a precious silky fabric, held with a belt and worn
over a shirt and pants. Later, in movies, Bahram will see men

wearing dressing gowns like this, but for now it adds to the magic of the place. Djam is standing under a lamp holding the little dog in his arms.

"I'm listening," he says.

He has a round face with fine features, and this makes him look gentle and kind. Bahram feels less intimidated. He stands to attention and recites almost in one breath: "Your very distinguished Majesty, Minister of Court, we are pupils from Djam School and we'll be finishing primary school this year and we'd like to continue our schooling but there's no high school in Gholhak, so we've come to ask if you would be kind enough to set up a seventh grade class in your school, please, your Majesty."

Ghassem has turned to stone. Hearing "Your very distinguished Majesty, Minister of Court" and meeting Djam in his garnet robe is quite an experience.

Djam is moved by this working-class child reciting his request; his words are awkward, it has to be said, but they have so much conviction. And anyway, Djam is amused that these boys seem to mistake him for the Shah. He stares at the boy for a moment, without a word. The patriot in him is touched: If all Iranians had this strength of will, Iran would be the greatest of nations.

Djam sets down his dog and Ghassem thinks, That's it, he's going to come and slap us, kick us, and throw us out.

"Follow me," Djam says, and he takes them into the house, across a wide corridor, and through a large living room decorated in European style, then opens the door to his office. Bahram follows him in but Ghassem and Siavosh wait in the doorway. Bahram notices two large paintings above the desk: portraits of the Shah and his father, Reza Shah.

Djam opens a box, takes out a card, picks up his pen, and writes a quick note.

"What's your name?" he asks Bahram.

"Bahram . . . "

"Come here, Bahram. Give this to your headmaster and you shall have your seventh grade."

Bahram takes the card, bows, and kisses Djam's hand. He has seen peasants doing this to dignitaries.

Before leaving the room, Bahram turns around and says in a voice quivering with emotion, "Thank you, your very distinguished Majesty."

Djam smiles and the boys leave. Djam thinks he has just done something good and noble, that this is his destiny. Bahram thinks this really is a roomy house.

T his is for you, sir."

"What is it?" asks the headmaster.

The short message is addressed to the Minister of Culture, and in it Djam asks him to open a seventh grade class at Djam School in Gholhak.

It is the first time Bahram has seen the headmaster lost for words. The man looks up, gazes into the distance for a moment, then puts the note in his pocket and keeps on walking.

Bahram takes his exams to graduate from sixth grade at the Shapour High School in Tadjrish. During the exam, the headmaster takes the proctor to one side to have a couple of words, one about Bahram, the other about Hassan Rahnama. These two boys have to get through: Bahram because he is his protégé and Hassan because of his knife. Hassan is the school big shot, and even the omnipotent headmaster is powerless against him. He is four years older than Bahram and he lays down the law at school. He takes *falak* beatings without turning a hair, and is quick to unsheathe his knife. Over the years Bahram has managed to soften him up by giving him dried fruit from home. Everyone has their own way of handling Hassan: Bahram with dried fruit, the headmaster by making sure he graduates each year, in the hopes he will finally leave.

Hassan Rahnama has to take sixth grade again but Bahram graduates successfully. As a reward, Talla buys him a watch, a West End watch.

Through Ghassem's father, who works at the Iran Cement

factory, Bahram learns that Saname has gone to Switzerland, to one of those boarding schools where the rich send their children for a good education, to learn fancy European manners and become high-ranking civil servants, doctors, lawyers, and the like. Bahram remembers one last time those footsteps of Saname's that he never heard . . .

Talla turned forty that year, and started to feel tired. She felt she would soon grow old and that there must be something she should do, one thing people did while they still had the strength. The last thing she needed to accomplish. So she thought about going back to see Ghamsar, visiting the land of her birth before it was too late. She liked the idea of going there with her son, to show him Ghamsar. Bahram was a sturdy child who worked hard at school, had his sixth grade graduation under his belt, and was just finishing eighth grade. He deserved to see the land of his ancestors.

Now that there were cars, more and more Ghamsaris came to Tehran, bringing with them dried fruits, rosewater, and news of family members and other villagers. Talla had heard that her mother had died, and later her father. She had wept for them and then forgotten them. But still the Ghamsaris came, reviving dead memories.

She mentioned the idea to Sardar, who gave his consent but made it clear that he needed to look after the land and livestock, and could not make the journey with her. Sardar had no desire to go back to Ghamsar, which had always been a prison to him. The mountains all around, no outlook, a blocked horizon. Where others saw paradise, he saw a cage. He had succeeded in Tehran, he had his own house, his animals, his radio, a son who could read . . . He would not be returning to Ghamsar. She could go if it made her happy, she could take her son with her to show him the village. But he, Sardar, would not be going and would give no other reason than that he had live-stock to tend.

"Say hello to everyone for me. Here, take this money and give it to the two imamzadehs."

Talla went to see the headmaster to ask permission for Bahram to be away for two weeks; she came with a pail of yogurt, some cream, and some eggs. She put all her gifts on the headmaster's desk and said, "Please, sir . . . "

They left in *Ordibehesht*, halfway through spring, so that they would reach Ghamsar in time for the Feast of the Rose. They traveled by car as far as Kashan, taking two seats in one of the cars that transported people between the capital and the country's other large cities. They sat together on the front seat. A family of five climbed in the back, two adults and three children. Throughout the trip the driver hummed popular songs and the children cried in the back. Talla was thrilled to see those immutable landscapes and the same fascinating route that had brought her to Tehran. But she preferred traveling on an ass's back.

In Kashan they spent the night in a caravanserai, and visited the city the next day. Talla was happy to be back in Kashan's bazaar and to lunch with her son in a café she thought she recognized, twenty-eight years on.

"Don't travel alone from Kashan to Ghamsar," Sardar had advised. "Pay someone to go and say you're coming, they'll come and fetch you." Talla's older brother would come for them.

Perched on an ass, Talla arrived back in Ghamsar. Having left as a young girl of twelve, she was back as a forty-year-old woman. Her face was deeply lined, grey hairs peeped from under her veil, and she had noticeably fewer teeth. She did not recognize her brother: He was twenty-two when she left but now she was reunited with an old man. Everyone she knew was old now. They gazed at each other with tenderness and astonishment. Talla's arrival meant they could gauge the passage of time. Talla saw herself in the mirror of their tired faces burned by the sun and the cold, in the crumpled, withered old skin of the women who had been her playmates when she was a little girl. And then she realized that she would not be growing old someday, she already had grown old. How the years had flown by!

Talla regretted making the trip. The moment she set foot in Ghamsar she could see nothing had changed, everything was in its rightful place, not so much as a tree had moved, no path had been rerouted. None of the new inventions that were taking over the city had reached this place. And everywhere she saw images of Havva and of their sacrificed youth. What a disturbing feeling it was to be back in the identical landscape of her childhood when she herself was old.

Only the Feast of the Rose succeeded in reminding her of the delights of her childhood and delivered her briefly from her heartache.

They made the return journey in stifling heat and a fraught atmosphere. Talla wept all the way to Tehran and, desperate to get back to his friends in Gholak, Bahram kept complaining he was bored. He had found nothing to do or talk about with the children in Ghamsar, strange creatures who did not go to school, could not read, had never heard of radio or movies, and looked inquisitively at the unfamiliar thing he wore on his wrist: his watch. And he had had enough of his mother's tears.

B ack in Ghamsar, Bahram is enthusiastic about returning to school. Before his trip, he went to see Djam for the third time. Djam granted them an eighth grade class last year, and is offering them a ninth grade this year. Djam is now a part of Bahram's life, and in his own small way the boy is part of his. They meet once a year, knowing that no familiarity of any sort is possible between them, not one superfluous word, one uncalled-for gesture. But they have a solid understanding and each plays his part. They play their roles together once a year, and at the end of the performance they are proud of each other.

On the last day of the academic year, the headmaster comes to find Bahram in his classroom and asks him to come with him. Bahram is unconcerned as he follows him along the corridor. He now knows that, for some mysterious reason, the headmaster is his protector. A peculiar relationship has developed between them, each owes something to the other, although Bahram does not fully understand this.

The headmaster sits in his chair and, for the first time, invites Bahram to sit down.

"I'm going to talk to you man-to-man today. I don't know how you managed to get Djam to set up a class for seventh grade, then eighth grade, and now ninth grade, but you should know that by having a ninth grade class this school has now officially become a high school. From the beginning of the next academic year, the primary school will be transferred into new buildings. And I can no longer be headmaster here because I would need a university degree to be headmaster of a high school, and I don't have one. So I've been invited to run the schools department at the ministry. I'm not complaining, in a way I'm becoming the headmaster of headmasters! Still, I'll be sad to leave this school, I watched it being built, I've run the place and it's now one of the best schools in the region."

He pauses a while to keep his emotions under control, then adds, "I thought I would change your fate and it's you who's changing mine."

Bahram feels awkward and does not know where to look. He lowers his head as much as he can. He feels so guilty he could cry.

"I'm sorry, sir."

"No, don't be! I have a wonderful promotion and you have your high school. And we both deserve it," the headmaster says, smiling affectionately.

It is the first time Bahram has seen him smile so genuinely. He really doesn't understand what's going on.

"Now listen, Bahram, you've been my best pupil since this school started. Not because of your grades—there are other pupils with excellent grades across all subjects—but because you have talent."

In that moment Bahram's drawings hanging in the headmaster's office take on a new dimension. The bird perched in a tree, hanging behind his chair just beneath the portrait of the Shah, suddenly sparkles. You can almost hear it sing. Only then does Bahram understand that that's what talent is. He has always been proud that the headmaster hangs his pictures in his office, but has thought all along that this was just because no one else in school did any drawing. To make the leap from there to acknowledging he has talent . . . that makes even his visits to Djam seem less exceptional. Bahram is an only child: He does not operate by hoping but by wanting, seeking, asking, and getting. Not that it makes him any happier, it is simply how things work. But at this moment his perception of himself makes a sudden shift: He feels the headmaster is marking him out as a prodigy.

"I want you to keep going with this, I want you to make the most of your talent, I want you to go to university. This country needs a well-educated elite, and I want you to be part of that. But when you achieve that—because you will achieve it—never forget where you're from. You're a child of the people, and educating the people will be our country's salvation. I've devoted my life to it. I could have been in trade and made much more money, traveled in Europe and driven a car. I chose to serve my country. Your parents have worked our country's land with their own hands, you belong to that hardworking people. Never forget to serve your country first, before yourself. I'm counting on you. I'll be hearing about you."

Bahram comes out of the headmaster's office thunderstruck. All his convictions, his relationship with society, with his country, and with himself have just been forged in that office. With a strange mix of narcissism and patriotism, he already feels he has reached the top of the ladder and has a mission to accomplish for his country. And it is his school headmaster, the highest authority in his young life, who has entrusted him with it.

G abr knocks at the door. Gabr is a Zoroastrian, a hunting man and a traveling salt salesman. He is a great strong man with a mane of hair and an abundant beard. He comes by from time to time and trades five or six pounds of salt for dairy products. It is early fall and this will be his last visit of the year. He disappears in winter, claiming he heads south. If Sardar is at home when he drops by, Gabr takes out the shotgun he keeps hidden in his saddle. Since Sardar sold his own shotgun to Ghamsar he rarely has the chance to touch one. He strokes the barrel, aims at an animal, and mimes pulling the trigger. And it makes both men happy.

Talla is preparing *ghormeh* for the winter. A couple of days ago Sardar killed a sheep; he skinned and gutted it, then jointed it and cleaned the meat. Talla boned the joints yesterday. This morning she is cutting up the meat and using a large cooking pot to mix it with well-salted mutton fat. She will leave it to cook for several hours, then she will preserve it in sheep's intestines she has been preparing over the summer. She takes the animal's rumen, blows into it until it is fully inflated, then leaves it to dry in the sun. When she has filled these pouches she hangs them from the ceiling of the upstairs room, which is not heated in winter. And all through the winter, whenever she needs meat to cook, she will take it from these pouches.

When Gabr knocks on the door, Talla's hands are covered in grease. Bahram is lying under the mulberry tree reading

Balzac's *Lost Illusions*. Talla asks him to go open the door, and Bahram grumbles, unwilling to put down his book.

Gabr asks whether his father is in. Bahram says he is so Gabr takes his hidden shotgun and asks Bahram to keep an eye on his donkey and his stock of salt. Bahram will be fifteen this year; he does not like taking orders from Gabr as if he were still a little boy. Irritated, he hunkers down in the shade of a tree, picks up pebbles, and starts lobbing them at the wall of the house opposite. The door suddenly opens and Bahram thinks it is someone coming to reprimand him for throwing stones, but three girls his age emerge from the building.

The house opposite belongs to Mirza and Mahtab-Khanoum; seven adjoining rooms forming a horseshoe shape around a central courtyard. Mirza and his family occupy two of the rooms and rent out the others to other families. They also have a chicken coop, and their tenants sometimes bring their own livestock and keep the animals in the yard. Stepping into their home feels a little like arriving at a caravanserai; the place is filled with an unbelievable number of people of all ages and animals. When Bahram sleeps on the roof in summer he hears them talking, shouting, and laughing, and then all at once the noise drops as if someone has announced a curfew, everyone stops talking, even the children fall silent. How odd, Bahram thinks. I'll go have a look one day, I'll climb the wall and watch them in secret, to see if someone gives the signal: "Okay, time's up, goodnight and no more noise."

Ever since he came to live here Bahram has spent time with the children from Mirza's house—both boys and girls. They often play together: football with the boys, hide-and-seek with the girls. When he was younger, he regularly fell in love with one or other of the girls and would come home and beg his mother, "Please go ask for so-and-so's hand, I want to marry her!"

There is a newcomer in this trio of girls coming out of the house. A girl with blue eyes! Braham abandons Gabr's donkey and follows them with a "hey, girls!" Talla, her name is. Another Talla! She has just moved in with her mother and sister. They have no father and her mother is Russian with golden hair and skin as white as milk. The memory of those German women tugs at Bahram's heart yet again.

He tells her she has the same name as his mother. It suits her, he thinks, because she has golden hair and Talla means "gold."

Bahram watches out for Talla all through the fall, but rarely has a chance to talk to her. Then comes winter, when everyone retreats indoors. The days grow shorter, it is icy cold, and parents do not let their children outdoors. People go to bed earlier, too, and Bahram lies dreaming in his bed. He imagines Talla in a swimming costume among the German women, and pictures himself standing beside her by the pool.

That winter nothing can take Bahram's mind off thoughts of Talla. Not even a mysterious assassination attempt on the Shah! Even though Mirza joins Sardar under the *korsi* every evening to listen to the radio, and the whole family hears Mohammad Reza Shah addressing the nation when he is discharged from hospital. Sardar and Mirza are very moved, and pray for him.

"The man who shot the Shah was carrying a membership card for Iran's Communist Party, the Toudeh, and a press card for an Islamic newspaper. That's why the Shah's banned the Toudeh Party and Ayatollah Kashani's been arrested," Mirza's son Mohsen tells them.

"Allahu Akbar!"

But Bahram hears neither the radio nor their comments; he is writing love poems.

With the arrival of spring, children come back out into the streets to play, and Bahram and Talla see each other again. That summer Bahram finds work on a farm, picking cherries for two tomans a day. Talla is proud that her son is working and earning money, and Bahram does it to make her happy. At work one day he finds some beautiful red apples under an apple tree, and puts two in his pocket to share with Talla. When he arrives home his mother notices his bulging pockets and asks him what he is hiding. His mother does not like the other Talla, and she justifies these feelings by telling herself the girl grew from a Russian seed, an infidel seed.

Bahram tells her Talla's father is Iranian and a Muslim; he is a Turk from Tabriz. He married Talla's mother when he was studying in Russia, then they lived in Tabriz, but after the war he had to follow the Russian army and flee to Russia because he had been a politician in Tabriz; there has been no news of him since. Talla's mother came here to find members of his family who, by contrast, fled Russia after the Communists came to power, and now live somewhere in Tehran. She hopes they will help and support her in her efforts to give her two daughters a worthy upbringing. But Talla is not interested in any of this. She wants to know what he has in his pockets.

"Red apples."

"Give them to me."

"No, they're for Talla. The other Talla."

This is Bahram's first real love, and Talla is well aware of it. How painful it is when your son draws away and loves another woman. And an infidel, too, with blue eyes, and the same name as her—it's more than she can bear. Talla confiscates the apples and, furious, Bahram tells he will not be going back to work on the farm.

He sulks for several days, shuts himself in his room on the upper floor, reading and drawing. But he is soon bored. Sardar suggests he go and work for Mash-Rahim at the grocery store. Bahram enjoys being on the other side of the counter and serving locals. And he wants to earn some money so that he and Talla can have photographs taken. He wants them to have a photo of each other.

For his visit to the photographer he wears his new suit, which dates from Norouz the same year. The photographer asks him to stand beside a column topped with a vase of flowers. He puts a white scarf around Bahram's neck and ties it carefully under his chin. He takes three shots: Bahram resting his elbow on the column, Bahram with his hand at his waist, and Bahram looking relaxed with his jacket unbuttoned. Bahram decides to give the Talla the one of him leaning on the column. He likes the effect: He looks good and his face has come out perfectly.

Talla gives him a picture of herself in exchange. In it her hair is scooped up into a chignon, she looks like a woman already. Bahram does not like it. He thinks she looks coquettish. He wants a photo that looks like her, he wants her as a young girl, the way she looks every day; he tells her so.

After a few weeks, when Bahram's mother can see her son is still resentful about the episode with the apples, she becomes more conciliatory and allows Talla to come to the garden and spend time with her son. They start making paper bags which they sell to tradesmen. They want to earn some money so Talla can go back to the photographer and have another photo taken, one that will appeal to Bahram. In the meantime, under the nest where a pair of nightingales come back every year to lay their eggs in Sardar and Talla's garden, Bahram kisses a girl for the first time. Her lips are soft and moist, and Bahram's hands tremble at her waist as much as his lips do on hers.

But then one evening the mayor of Gholhak holds a reception in his garden. The music can be heard from a long way away. Bahram knows Talla and her family have been invited. He wonders why the mayor has invited them, so he and Ghassem decide to go see for themselves. They climb onto the garden wall and Bahram catches sight of Talla dancing with the mayor's son—cheek to cheek, as they say. He jumps down from the wall, runs home, finds a stick, and comes back to hide in the shadows outside the mayor's house. He wants to beat the mayor's son and Talla when they come out. He is so angry he is determined to split their heads open, the pair of them. He stays by the door until midnight when his now-frantic mother comes to find him and bring him home by force.

When Talla came to see him the next day he immediately drove her away. She could not understand this sudden fury and he gave her no explanation. He never forgave her that dance, he tore up the photo of her with her topknot and never spoke to her again. He had planned to marry her and in exchange she had dishonored him by dancing with someone else. No man could accept that. Even Talla senior tried to intervene in the younger Talla's favor when the girl came to her weeping. There was nothing for it, he would not change his mind.

The summer came to an end and Talla, her mother, and her younger sister, whose name was Toutti, left the area to go live in Tehran, and Bahram never heard of them again . . .

The month of *Muharram* comes around. In the Islamic lunar calendar the tenth day of *Muharram* is *Ashura Day*, when the martyrdom of Imam Hossein is remembered. When Sardar settled in Shemiran he sometimes drove his flock to Varamine, a small village to the south of Tehran, for their summer grazing. In those days *Muharram* fell in the summer. He never saw a more spectacular ceremony than *Ashura* in Varamine. It took ten men to carry the *allams*, ceremonial constructions decorated with feathers and candles, and there were sumptuous *Ashura* costumes representing Imam Hossein and his martyrdom. Sardar has described these splendors to Mirza and suggests he comes along this year with their sons: Ali-Agha, Mohsen, and Bahram.

They spend two days wrapped up in the rituals for *Ashura,* which are especially poignant in Varamine. On the first evening, men go to the great *Tekyeh* hall, where the walls are hung with black fabric as a mark of mourning. They sing *Muharram* hymns and beat their chests, first raising their hands to heaven then thumping them rhythmically onto their hearts. The pounding sound of palms smacking on bodies reverberates for hours on end. Dressed entirely in black, they beat themselves and chant in a trance, and tears flow over their cheeks. Women in black chadors sit weeping along the sides. Tears glint amid a sea of black.

The next day they join the procession through the streets of the small town. In the fervor of hymns and swaying *Ashura* banners, men flagellate themselves with chains, and Sardar is completely carried away by the emotion. The dense, black crowd, the river of tears, and above them the brightly colored feathers on the *allams* beat time to the rhythm of the wind.

Bahram, on the other hand, is captivated by bewitching eye contact with a young girl who wears her chador with casual nonchalance. At seventeen he has grown into an irresistibly good-looking young man. Tall, slim, broad-shouldered, bare-chested with tan skin and hair so black it gleams in the sun like gold, he is the very image of virility as he beats his chest with exhilaration. They lose sight of each other and then make eye contact again. And the wind blows the young woman's chador, now disguising and now revealing the outline of her body; and she certainly knows it. With all the intensity of the forbidden, their complicity is instant as well as unwise, but the crowd around them rolls on like a wave and separates them.

That same evening, when Bahram is out in the square where *Ashura* plays are being performed, he spots her sitting on the roof of a house. She sees him, too, disappears for a moment, then comes back and throws him a pebble wrapped in a piece of paper. Bahram darts over to pick it up. She has written her name and address on it. Bahram stows the note in his pocket and goes back to where he was.

Early the next morning, the five of them are standing beside the bus which will take them back to Shemiran. While waiting for it to leave, Sardar and Mirza smoke their pipes. Bahram and his friends are chatting quietly when the boy from the hostel where they spent the night appears from nowhere, running breathlessly toward them.

"Run, run, they want to kill you!" he shrieks at Bahram and vanishes as quickly as he came.

"What's going on? What did he say?" asks Sardar.

"Run, they're coming to kill you!" Ali-Agha tells him.

Almost as he says it, a troop of several dozen men comes

running toward them, shouting and issuing threats: Bahram was seen picking up the girl's note yesterday . . . this boy who is not from this town has sinned, he wanted to seduce a girl during *Ashura*, he must be punished. The men are descending on Bahram and he decamps at great speed. He can hear them behind him, and runs without looking back. Their baying gives him wings. He keeps running even when he can no longer hear them and has definitely shaken them off. He eventually stops on a plain in the middle of nowhere, and cannot see a soul whichever way he looks. He then starts walking north but when he reaches Tehran he realizes he has absolutely no money and cannot take the bus. He just keeps walking all the way to Shemiran and arrives home after nightfall. His father is hunkered down under the mulberry tree, his mother sitting on the step to the terrace.

"What time do you call this? Why didn't you come home with your father?" Talla scolds.

Bahram grasps that his father has not told her the story.

"Come and sit down, I'll get you something to eat," she softens.

The moment her back is turned Sardar beckons Bahram over.

"You have sinned. You need to go see the ayatollah to ask what you must do to secure God's forgiveness."

Sardar does not say another word, he is relieved to have his son back safe and sound. He ran behind the crowd to try to help Bahram, but quickly realized that his son's turn of speed meant he was safe from his pursuers, so he himself went back to the bus feeling reassured. But furious. He had suffered the greatest shame of his life in front of Mirza and all those other men.

"It's just a youthful little sin," Mirza soothed when they were on the bus. "All Bahram did was pick up a note from a wayward girl . . . it's not as if he touched her, thank God! God forgive him! The ayatollah will know what he needs to do."

And then, in front of Sardar, Mirza told his own sons not to mention this incident in Gholhak, not to Talla nor to their own mother, not to anyone. And the boys held their tongues.

Bahram collapses as soon as he has finished eating. Tired from running and walking so far, but mostly overwhelmed by shame. He has never known his father to be so angry with him. Sardar rarely comments on his son's life or actions, and almost never reprimands him. His anger is expressed not in words but in the intensity with which he furrows his brow. And yet, the unsettling glances from the girl with the note were still more powerful than Sardar's furious expression.

Two days later when Bahram was meant to be going to see the ayatollah, he put the girl's note in his pocket and went to the center of Tehran, to Monirieh, which was a wealthy residential neighborhood in the days of the Qajar. He walked all around it and eventually found the road named on the piece of paper. But as he walked closer he noticed a group of hulking young men sitting on the ground. Bahram did not dare venture further.

Two days went by and then, taking his courage in his hands, he set off for Monirieh again. On his way there he bought two chicks and asked for them to be put into a cardboard box with little holes so they could breathe. The big strong men were still there, sitting in the same place. He went up to them and asked them to show him which house was Mr. Makhmalchi's. They gave him no trouble and pointed it out for him right away.

Bahram knocks at the door and Mahine herself comes to open it. She gives a happy little yelp of surprise and invites him in. Her family must be rich because it is a beautiful big house. It is built in traditional style with a first "public" building, which in Qajar times would be the preserve of men, but he sees no one here; then there is an inner courtyard and a second "private" building intended for women. This family seems to use the first building for receiving guests and the second for everyday life.

Mahine is surrounded by her mother, her grandmother, her little sister, two maids, and an old servant who works as a handyman. They are in the guests' living room and the women, who are still wearing their chadors, offer Bahram a cordial and some fresh fruit. Then insist he stay for lunch. The maids spread the cloth on a large carpet on the ground in the courtyard. The two chicks Bahram has given to Mahine run around the garden, clearly happy with their new home.

Before lunch, Bahram and Mahine find themselves alone for a moment. Mahine has been holding her chador under her chin with one hand but she lets it go: It falls open, revealing her torso and a glimpse of her breasts where her blouse is unbuttoned. All Bahram saw of her during Ashura were her big brown eyes; now he is free to study every inch of her alluring face, on display for him alone. She has high cheekbones, a small nose, and a large mouth with an upturned upper lip. Her dusky skin gleams healthily and she has full breasts. At the sound of footsteps, Mahine pulls her chador closed again and Bahram looks away.

They all have lunch and then take tea. When it comes to siesta time, Bahram gets up to leave, and Mahine sees him to the door. Bahram tells her that sadly nothing is possible between them, they are not from the same social background, and Mahine's father would never give her as a wife to a boy like him. Mahine laughs out loud and says this is nothing to do with marriage, she is a widow and this house belongs to her. Bahram would never have guessed, she's so young!

For the young of Iran, siesta time has always been a time of frivolity and transgression. Instead of opening the door to let him out, Mahine takes Bahram's hand and leads him to another room. She locks the door and allows her chador to drop to the floor. Bahram is caught out, not quite sure what will happen next. And Mahine is in a hurry, because of her desire, because they have so little time, and because she is afraid someone might come. She grabs Bahram's hand, slips it inside her bra, and presses it against her breast. There is something in Mahine's eyes that Bahram has never seen before. Their breathing accelerates. She frees her hair and her breasts with sensuous, salaciously graceful moves. Bahram cannot believe his eyes: she is beautiful and satanic—she is the evil people wish for, the sin they dream of. She hitches up her skirt, takes off her panties, and offers herself. Bahram thinks he might pass out, his heart is beating faster than when he runs the one hundred meters. She is in a paroxysm of desire, cannot bear for Bahram to take his hands from her breasts; her own hands are undoing his pants while her scalding lips burn they way over the young man's face. She asks him to take her, all of her. Bahram does not know what to do. So she does it for him. Carried away by Mahine's tempestuous passion, Bahram shudders and sways under the ardently writhing body of this woman he will never see again. It does not last long. But long enough for Bahram to explore the mystery of a woman's libido. When his man's thirst has been assuaged, Mahine smiles sweetly as a fairy and briefly strokes his panting chest while he kisses her hand before leaving.

On the way home to Gholhak he feels like whooping for joy: A diabolical but sublime virtuoso has just—very graciously—led him over the threshold into manhood. What he cannot know is that life not only surprised him today, but more importantly it gave him the greatest of gifts. He has just tasted carnal love, and with that very first experience he discovered something that many men on this earth never know: a woman's pleasure.

As soon as he is back in Gholhak he goes to the ayatollah to ask for an audience, and is granted one the next day. The ayatollah studied in Nadjaf and has a reputation as a fair and moderate man. He sits on a cushion, alone at the far end of a large room. He is wearing a black turban, a sign that he is descended from the Prophet, and has a splendid white beard. Bahram comes in, kisses his hand, sits in front of him, and tells him about his sin: he looked at a girl and accepted a note from her during the *Ashura* ceremony. The ayatollah tells him to fast for two days, to buy two kilos of dates and hand them out in the street. He tells him he is young and has committed a young man's sin, and God will forgive him. Then the ayatollah says he can go. Bahram stays sitting, his head lowered, still silent. The ayatollah quickly understands, and suspects something more serious. His face changes, his expression hardens.

"Do you have something else to tell me?"

Bahram feels he must point out that she was a widow.

"And what else?"

Bahram does not reply.

"God alone is your judge," the ayatollah tells him, "but if you came to ask my advice, I would tell you to fast for an entire month and never go back there, and if God chooses to he will forgive you. Now you must face him alone."

Bahram stands up, kisses the ayatollah's hand again, and leaves.

Sardar notices his son fasting and thinks a month of abstinence a little severe for picking up a scrap of paper, but the ayatollah knows what he's doing, it must be serious in the eyes of the faith. Talla is intrigued by this sudden piety, and knows it is hiding something. She questions Bahram and Sardar, but does not get to the truth. Men show solidarity in the face of women's curiosity, which tries to probe their secrets.

IV
FIROUZEH,
A WISE MAN'S DREAM

On *Mehr* 1st, 1330, the first day of fall, a cool wind sweeps through Baharestan Square in Tehran, swirling around the National Assembly buildings and Sepahsalar Mosque. Bahram is standing shyly under the porch of Dar-ul Funun Polytechnic College, its name inscribed in Arab script on a strip of Persian blue ceramic. On the lapel of his jacket he wears a white ribbon bearing the words "Nationalize Iranian Oil." Dar-ul Funun is a symbol of modern Iran, the country's first institution of higher education, and it is currently a prestigious high school. It is about to accept Bahram as a student, and he mops the nervous sweat from his brow before finally stepping inside.

Dar-ul Funun was founded exactly a hundred years earlier by Amir Kabir, chancellor to Naer al-Din Shah Qajar, for the teaching of medicine and the sciences. It was inaugurated in 1230 in the presence of the Shah, Iranian and European teachers, and thirty student princes. When Reza Shah created Tehran University in 1312, Dar-ul Funun became the capital's most reputable public high school.

Gholhak's Djam High School did not manage to open a tenth grade class. It would have needed ten students to set one up, but most of them left school after graduating ninth grade. Even Ghassem left to become a railway administrator, thereby realizing his father's improbable dream. Bahram continued his studies at Shapour High School in Tadjrish to the north of Shemiran. A brilliant student, he has bowed to pressure from his teachers, who felt he belonged at Dar-ul Funun, and he has enrolled here for the last year of high school in the hopes of securing the most renowned school diploma in the country.

Bahram stands in Dar-ul Funun's square courtyard that first day, surrounded by buildings with tall arches, in the shade of big trees, at a crossing of the pathways, which—as in every Persian garden—lead to an ornamental pond with water streaming from a *qanat*; his first thought is for Amir Kabir. When Bahram and Talla went to Ghamsar they visited Kashan and the Fin Gardens with their rectangular ponds, the site of Amir Kabir's assassination two weeks after the inauguration of Dar-ul Funun. It is said that Kabir's mother extracted the order for this killing from Naser al-Din Shah one drunken night. Bahram remembers the turquoise tiles in the pools, the small now-empty pond in which Amir Kabir bathed for the last time, his blood spilling from his veins after he asked his assassins the favor of choosing the instrument of his death . . . then he thinks of Naser al-Din Shah's assassination and of Shah-Abdol-Azim. He has heard that, by some irony of fate or the serendipity of the place, having been struck by the bullet he took three steps back and fell into the Jayran room—the room he had given the same name as his favorite wife in his harem. He also remembers that Naser al-Din Shah refused entry to Dar-ul Funun to commoners; only the sons of princes and noblemen belonged there.

"What am I doing here?" he thinks, and yet he is aware of how things have evolved in those hundred years. But he also knows that the significance of social rank will never be erased from these walls or these paving stones, or his own heart. He knows he is the most brilliant, most gifted boy in Gholhak, but that he is and always will be the son of a peasant. Trapped by his ambivalent destiny, he can see two possible outcomes: either he will flee pathetically, expelling himself before he is expelled on an order from the king or—worse—the king's steward; or he will be singing the victory hymn while brandishing his sword and Spartan shield (in moments of vanity like this it always the image of a Spartan that comes to mind, like something he saw in a film whose title he has forgotten).

It strikes him that everything here is absurd, Dar-ul Funun is the crossroads of all those broken trajectories: of people tragically propelled off course by events no one could have predicted. He feels intuitively that the chaos will not stop there, more unforeseeable factors will come to toy with fate. He thinks that when God created this country he made its first characteristic "tragedy," the song of sacrifice, in the most Greek sense of the word. Perhaps that is what constitutes the curse of Alexander—a figure he hates to the deepest fiber of his being.

Did Mossadegh have these same thoughts when, not long after this, he stood before the United Nations Security Council pleading the case for Iran? Was Mossadegh nervous as he stepped into the UN? Was the situation within his scope? Or did he think only of the goal that his personal trajectory was meant to achieve?

S ince Parliament voted in the nationalization of Iranian oil, since Mossadegh became prime minister in the spring of this year, life has completely changed for Gholhakis. Amid a turmoil of ideas and debates, Gholhak has seen its young men transformed into heroes setting out to achieve sovereignty for their country, whatever the cost. But they do not go blindly; they read and listen, discuss and concur. Even though they are united behind Mossadegh in opposing the English, each has his own opinion. Some feel he should have negotiated a 50/50 division of assets as the Americans did in Arabia; others that it is a question of principles, that the arrogance of the English means only nationalization could appease the Iranians' anger. Still others feel the English might have accepted nationalization in exchange for the compensation Mossadegh was offering them, that they might then have managed to negotiate fifty percent exploitation rights. But they know that the refinery in Abadan with its 37,000 employees is peerless, the biggest in the world, so this was a question of prestige for the English. Bahram believes what Mossadegh believes; his support is unfaltering.

Since Mossadegh came to power Bahram has stopped reading Hugo, Balzac, and Jules Verne; he now reads the quantities of pamphlets published by political parties on every possible political subject. So many young men are consumed with what they read in these pamphlets and by the leaders of their day. Bahram is a fervent admirer of Mossadegh, but also of Hossein

Fatemi, the Minister for Foreign Affairs, who is his role model, his idol—he wishes he could be him. There are plenty more he admires, including Abol-Hassan Amidi-e Nouri, founder of the *Dad* newspaper and a member of the National Front, who lives in Gholhak. Bahram sometimes sees him in the street and greets him respectfully. He would like the man to notice the "Nationalize Iranian Oil" ribbon stitched to his lapel. Surely he does notice it, and reciprocates the friendly greeting.

T his ship will sail or fail through these eddies . . . a poet once said.

Bahram has just listened to Mossadegh on the radio making a speech to the United Nations to defend the nationalization of Iranian oil because the English have brought the case before the UN Security Council. He heads upstairs, sits on the window ledge, and puts his mind to memorizing Mossadegh's words while drawing a picture of the garden. As is the custom now, he learns by heart anything that he thinks is important. He is still too young to have his own ideas; he absorbs and repeats what is said in the papers, in books, and by politicians . . . And drawing is his companion when he is concentrating like this. He draws the mulberry tree, the pond, and the little ginger kitten he has just adopted to replace his old cat who died two months ago. A huge black cat appears out of nowhere and launches itself at the kitten. Bahram yells and the cat runs away, but the kitten stays sprawled on the ground. Bahram races downstairs to help it, and the mewling kitten manages to get back to its feet but its hind legs no longer work, its spine is broken. Bahram backs away. His parents come hurrying over and Bahram asks his mother to take the kitten away, he can't bear to see it in this state. Sardar kills the kitten swiftly to spare it further suffering, then puts the little body in a sack and removes it. Bahram returns to his room and Talla goes up after him to console him, but he rejects her attempts. She heads back downstairs but warns him to beware the curse of cats:

"This happened just after Mossadegh's speech, it's a bad omen for him. That's how things will end for Mossadegh. Someone far more powerful than him will catch him unawares and break him in two. Don't get too attached to Mossadegh like you were attached to that kitten!" But the harm is done, and Bahram will remember his mother's words: the curse of cats.

Nevertheless Mossadegh went on to win his case before the UN, whose decision was not final pending a conclusion from the court in the Hague.

Bahram is to spend only an uncomfortable three months at Dar-ul Funun. He is eighteen, the age when an adolescent becomes a man. But all the signs are that he must not become a man in the tradition of his inheritance, he must be fulfilled by breaking with that continuity. This is what they all want, his father, the headmaster of Djam School, everyone. Except him. He accepts it but also rejects it. A part of him rejects it. He now goes to Tehran every day; he needs to break away from Shemiran and the benign surroundings of his childhood. Particularly as this is an era that calls for fighters, for rebels; he must choose his camp. And this transition can take place only with all the pain of change.

Halfway through a lesson in the late fall he feels a stab of pain, falls from his chair, and lies unconscious on the floor. He is taken to hospital: appendicitis. He has had pain in his lower abdomen for a month but the local doctor in Gholhak could find nothing. He will be kept in for the night and given an emergency operation in the morning. The staff ask him how to contact his parents. Bahram tells them to call Gholhak's main telephone exchange, and ask them to pass the word on to the grocer whose shop is near the exchange—he will go and tell Bahram's parents.

Talla is given the news. News is always conveyed in the same way here whether it's the death of the king or Bahram's appendicitis: Someone arrives, always in a tearing hurry, and announces the information loudly and clearly.

"*Ya ghamar-e bani hashem!*" Talla cries, and starts beating her head and pulling her hair. Neighbors come running, lots of them. Sardar comes home and finds his wife collapsed in their arms. He thinks once again that he has lost his son. When he hears the news he is angry.

"Come on, come on, he's not dead!"

He wants to know where Bahram is. No one knows; the boy who relayed the information said only that he was in the hospital. Where was the boy from? From the grocery store. Sardar goes to see the grocer but he does not know either; he was simply asked to let them know their son was in the hospital. At the telephone exchange they have no idea, the operator who took the call has ended her shift and gone home. Where does she live? Sardar is told the address, and he goes straight there. She does not know either, she was given no details. In fact, all anyone has done is play his or her part it this little performance. The operator who took the message ran to the grocery store herself to pass on the news, then went back to the exchange and announced it to everyone there before repeating the facts back at home. The grocer called his son and told him to run and tell Talla, and he then informed all the customers who came by, right up until Sardar himself turned up. The boy ran to give the information to Talla, and to everyone he met both on the way and on the way back. And Talla screamed so loudly that all the neighbors heard the news. All of Gholhak now knows.

Sardar sits down outside the operator's house and wonders what to do. He decides the best solution is to go to the police station, you never know. The duty officer is a good man. He advises Sardar to go home and wait because the hospital is bound to call again. But first he should stop by the telephone exchange and ask them if they could, if the opportunity arises, make a note of the hospital's name for him. This is what Sardar does, and he arrives home tired and anxious, and has to contend with Talla's lamentations all night.

At dawn the eminent surgeon Dr. Hafezi operates on Bahram. Not having seen his parents, the young man is very afraid as he is taken to the operating theater. He cries and the surgeon comforts him kindly.

"Come on, my boy, it's nothing. I'm going to operate on you and you'll be on your feet in no time. But don't you go getting killed in one of these demonstrations afterward! Don't go spoiling my work!"

Bahram comes out alive, but never goes back to Dar-ul Funun.

He continues to complain of back pain and goes from doctor to doctor, but no one can find an explanation for his pain. At high school he is constantly the sick student, the absentee. He spends most of his time in bed reading the manifestoes that the political parties publish every day. The only outings he makes are to local meetings where all the talk is of nationalizing oil.

In late spring an ageing doctor tells him, "You're no sicker than I am, my boy. Your problem isn't in your body but your mind."

With that one sentence, the doctor cures him. At last someone who understands him. Bahram immediately gets out of bed and decides to sit for his school diploma exam. Without any preparation; there is no time for that. He does his best but comes away disappointed. He does not even envisage attending the oral exams. He persuades himself it doesn't matter, he can start over next year, he'll get his diploma.

For now the only thing that matters is that Mossadegh has made his speech before the court in the Hague, and they have rejected the English plea, saying it is outside their competence to judge a conflict between the Iranian state and a private company, the Anglo-Iranian Oil Company, rather than the United Kingdom.

Every afternoon, silence descends on Gholhak. Shops and offices close at noon, and everyone goes home, has lunch, and then takes a sacrosanct siesta—adults take it willingly, children by force, and even pets go along with them. There is not a sound to be heard, no footsteps or whisperings, not even the rustle of leaves: Silence reigns.

Bahram is having his siesta too, under the mulberry tree as usual. The ants that live at the foot of the tree march over him in single file. He can feel them on his arm, it is part of his routine and theirs. He leaves them to it; sometimes he tries to count them with his eyes closed, and falls asleep.

But on this particular afternoon the sound of the door knocker disturbs the Amir family's siesta and all their neighbors'.

"Bahram! Bahram!" someone cries from the far side of the door.

Bahram sits up, brushes off the ants, and says, "Come in, Darra."

Darra is a boy from Zargandeh, a small village near Gholhak. He and Bahram met at a meeting of the Shemiran cell of the Iranian Workers' Party. Bahram, who mixes with various groups but has not opted decisively for one or the other, went on the invitation of a neighbor, Ebrahim Soltani, who runs the cell. At the moment he likes to think of himself as a member of the National Front, without officially adhering to one of its factions.

Darra is a year younger than Bahram; he is dark with blue eyes and a dazzling lust for life, not someone who can go unnoticed, like Bahram himself, who is beginning to look like a movie actor. Darra was soon impressed by his presence and eloquence, and is now a devoted, unfailing friend.

Newspapers are delivered to Shemiran at around two in the afternoon, while the inhabitants are resting, so they wake to fresh news.

Darra is waving a newspaper. He bought it out of curiosity to see the list of this year's students who have been awarded their diplomas, even though—other than Bahram—he knows no one who might possibly feature on it.

"Bahram, you got your diploma!" he announces.

Bahram cannot believe his eyes, his name is right there on the list: Bahram Amir, son of Sardar, born in Gholhak, ID card number 1.

This is how Bahram hears the news that he is the first ever inhabitant of Gholhak to be awarded his diploma.

That year's diplomas were soon nicknamed the Oil Diplomas. Malicious gossips claimed that everyone who sat the exams was given a diploma, that Mossadegh gave them out left, right, and center as a reward for coming out in favor of him and supporting his policy to nationalize oil.

A week later, on *Tir* 25th, 1331, came sudden news: Mossadegh had resigned. Bahram ran over to Ebrahim's house. It was true, he had called through to Tehran, Mossadegh really had resigned, the Shah had not accepted his suggested candidate for Minister of War. The *bazaari* had already shut up their stalls and workshops.

"People just won't let this happen," Ebrahim said passionately.

The Shah immediately appointed the experienced politician Ahmad Ghavam, sometimes called Ghavam el-Saltaneh, as prime minister. Ghavam started his mandate by announcing a new era of governance for the country, instantly inflaming the Iranian political scene.

The next day Bahram stayed glued to the radio until Darra arrived.

"I just came back from Tehran. People are going to demonstrate in the streets all the way from the bazaar to the Parliament building. Civil servants have decided to stop work, so have railway workers and even bus drivers. I almost had to come home on foot. Luckily someone in a car took pity on me."

The National Front appealed to all Iranians to demonstrate on *Tir* 30th. Communists in the Toudeh Party, the country's most significant political organization, also encouraged all its supporters to participate in this major demonstration. And Ayatollah Kashani, head of the religious reformists, openly professed his opposition to Ghavam. All the local young men were saying they would join in the protest.

Early on the morning of *Tir* 30th, Darra came to Bahram's house with a beaming smile and bursting with enthusiasm.

"Let's go!"

Bahram hesitated, trying to wriggle out of it. It was not that he doubted the cause—he certainly didn't, Mossadegh was his god on earth, and he was a fervent supporter of nationalizing oil—but Bahram liked things on a more intimate scale, between friends, those he chose, among whom he shone . . . He thought of himself more as a Mossadegh or a Fatemi. Now he felt he understood what the headmaster of Djam School expected of him: to be that sort of man, educated, cultivated, a great orator, and someone with true presence. Which meant large demonstrations and the anonymity of a crowd had little appeal for him . . . But Darra insisted and Bahram did not want to appear cowardly.

"Let's go," he said eventually.

J ust through Shemiran Gate, Tehran seems dead. They are surprised by the calm, and wonder whether the battle is over. They head toward the city center, and the outer neighborhoods feel empty. They walk in the blazing midsummer sunlight, the air is dry, the heat searing, and the light intense. They are wearing immaculate white shirts, Bahram has a watch on his wrist, a fountain pen hooked to the pocket of his shirt, and a sheet of white paper folded in four in the back pocket of his pants. Darra emptied his pockets before leaving.

All of a sudden they come face-to-face with two army tanks blocking their way. So that's it. Bahram can see armed soldiers behind the tanks, and remembers Dr Hafezi's words: "Don't you go getting killed in one of these demonstrations! Don't go spoiling my work."

An incalculable number of people gradually appear from the silence of the city, as if emerging from underground passages. Bahram cannot understand how they failed to see them on their way here.

Seven hours later when Bahram and Darra walk back through Shemiran Gate in the opposite direction, Bahram's shirt is black with dust, his watch is broken, his pen lost, and the sheet of paper has fluttered away. Darra has a torn sleeve and a split eyebrow. The city has been in turmoil for five hours. People of every leaning brandished their parties' banners, Communists rubbing shoulders with religious figures, *bazaaris*, and National Front militants. They were all there, everyone from Tehran and its neighboring communities, even from outlying provinces. And the army fired shots, Bahram and Darra ran away, and then, pursued by mounted troops, they ran again. Some demonstrators fell, and they helped them back to their feet. At one point Bahram was struck so hard with a truncheon he was propelled forward several yards. It was a brutal blow. He could not tell who had struck him or when. He saw other people falling and felt invulnerable himself. The young believe they are immortal; that is their strength.

When Bahram got back to his feet he saw Darra grappling with a soldier who had him by the neck. His pride wounded, Bahram launched himself at the soldier, kicking him aggressively and managing to tear Darra from his clutches. Furious and contorted with pain, the soldier took out his pistol and pointed it at them. Darra came closer to him and looked him in the eye.

"Shoot if you're a man," he said. "Shoot your fellow countryman, go on, shoot, and live with it to the end of your days."

The two of them stood motionless, eyeballing each other. The heroism of this scene galvanized Bahram.

"Yes, and shoot twice!" he said, coming to stand beside Darra and not really thinking what he was doing. "But before you do, have a good look at our faces so they can haunt you as long as you live. If you like I'll give you my address so you'll know where we're buried. Come and visit our graves every Friday with your children and tell them why you killed us. Now, if you're a man, shoot."

The three men froze for a moment as if time were crystallized over them. Then the soldier looked around and saw all the faces watching him. There is no telling what went through his head, whether he was afraid of being lynched on the spot, whether he was shamed by the young men's courage, whether he was aware this was an unequal battle despite his pistol, or perhaps he suddenly embraced the cause . . . He put away his weapon, took off his military cap and jacket, and, amid the cheers of onlookers, he melted into the crowd. Many other soldiers did the same thing. So many, in fact, that after five hours their commander was afraid of widespread mutiny and ordered his troops back to the barracks: The battle was over.

Bahram and Darra are heading home, the Shah will recall Mossadegh, and a new era will begin.

When Bahram arrives home that evening, Gholhak has that wet-soil smell of a freshly watered garden. Talla and Sardar are sitting outside their front door. Someone brought the news to them: The Shah instructed the use of firearms and cannons in Tehran, there were deaths. Talla cried, "*Ya ghamar-e bani hashem!*" and ran from house to house all over the neighborhood looking for Bahram. To his friends' houses, his classmates'. But every boy in Gholhak had disappeared.

"They're in Tehran, all of them, that's where they are," people told her. Then Talla ran all the way to Sardar's fields, but he did not know what to say. Talla beat her own head and still Sardar could not think what to do. They strayed through Gholhak's streets trying to find news, Talla even stopped cars on Shermiran Road. Tehran was in chaos, was all anyone could tell them. In the end Sardar dragged Talla home to wait and, exhausted by her hysteria, Talla let herself be led. They ended up sitting here.

They have been sitting here for three hours. Talla is praying, reciting the same verses from the Koran on a loop, in a trance. Sardar is trying to think about what is going on in this country that is swallowing up his son. He tries to remember what has been said on the radio over the last few days. As usual, there were words he did not understand so he imagined meanings for them based on the tone of voice and reached sometimes wildly wrong conclusions about what was being said. But he certainly grasped that Mossadegh had resigned, and claimed to be resigning so His Royal Majesty could appoint a prime minister of his choosing. Sardar thought this was a pleasant, courteous gesture, so why was everyone going to Tehran, and why was the Shah killing people? Has he gone mad? He thinks this thought very softly, really very quietly, afraid the Shah might read his mind. He thinks the Shah need only choose a prime minister and leave everyone in peace. He looks away into the distance but there is no one coming. Time goes by, Sardar starts to doubt, and his faith in life falters. He imagines his son's body being brought to him.

When Bahram appears, Talla shrieks and beats her chest. Sardar hides his tears of joy. Talla wails that she nearly died, that she spent hours looking for him, wandering around like a madwoman. Bahram knows she will not understand, but for his own satisfaction he tells her that when the Spartans went to war their mothers handed them their shields and told them to come back "behind it or on it."

"And I'm coming back with it," he tells her. Then he looks over to Sardar, who does understand.

"God keep you," his father says.

Bahram goes into the house and behind him he can hear Talla berating Sardar, "who doesn't know how to control his own son."

The heat is unlivable, more than forty degrees in the shade. The shade is exactly where Bahram is, fighting a fever that first took hold the day before. This morning his mother has drawn water from the well every hour and bathed his feet in cool water. It is not a violent fever, just an annoying one.

At noon someone knocks at the door.

"Come in," Talla cries.

"Hello," says Darra and then, seeing Bahram lying under the mulberry tree in his underwear, he adds, "but what are you doing?"

"I'm not going."

"What! Are you crazy!"

"I have a fever, I'm sick, I can't go."

It is the day of the national university entrance exams. Bahram has signed up to sit for the humanities exam. He would like to study history. If he is admitted he will follow a course in history and geography because the two disciplines are currently taught as a single subject.

But Bahram does not have the strength to go through the process . . . Deep down he would like to spend the rest of his life under this mulberry tree. Why go any further when life is so wonderful here! This is a protest fever. Sitting those exams and being accepted would mean leaving this behind, and he resists that prospect like a child. Tough luck for everyone who's put their hopes in him, all the Gholhakis who've treated him differently since he passed his diploma. He'll easily find some administrative job in Gholhak or Tadjrish, and he'll go to Tehran only for the movies or the cafés and restaurants . . . But Darra is not giving up; he volunteered to accompany him the day before and he is not backing down.

"What the hell does this mean? Let's see . . . you don't have all that much of a fever . . . don't you see? If you don't take these exams today, what are you going to do for the next year? You'll waste a year doing nothing and it'll just be harder for you to sit for the exams next year. Come on, come on, that's not going to happen, get up, get dressed, we're going. You want to go to university, you've told me that a thousand times, so you're going to sit for these exams. Otherwise you'll regret it . . . "

Darra is right, he would regret it. Bahram sits for the exam despite his fever and lack of motivation, and he passes with flying colors: He is placed sixteenth of the forty candidates who are accepted to the history and geography course in the faculty of humanities at Tehran's very prestigious university.

The headmaster of Djam School is first to know the results of the entrance exam; he sends him a congratulatory card full of encouragement for the future. He addresses the card to Mr. Bahram Amir—the most handsome reward.

On the first day of fall in 1331, when Harry S. Truman was president of the United States, Joseph Stalin was still very much in power, Sir Winston Churchill was back home, and they were all preparing to winter in the tentative peace of a world cut in two, favoring a hundred cold wars over one heated war, Bahram first went to university to study history, very aptly. At this point Iran was democratic, communist, socialist, totalitarian, religious, secular, and fundamentalist, and it was simultaneously pro-British, pro-American, pro-Soviet, in love with Hollywood, westernized, and faithful to its traditions. All these at once, and more. And in that chaos of ideologies and beliefs, everyone tried to devise a makeshift statement in clothing, a symbol of adhesion to—or rejection of—all or part of what inevitably happened: clashes between these factions.

At nightfall, though, they all withdrew from the flux of the outside world and returned to their civilized, loving, unchanging homes. They gathered together with glasses of tea that were constantly refilled because they could hold so little, and these glasses held so little precisely so they could justify this endless ritual of being refilled with tea served meticulously in the correct color, in the correct quantities, at the correct temperature, and accompanied by the correct courtesies. Amid this warmth and intimacy, people shared their treasure troves of stories, rumors, paranoia, and suspicion. Only one thing was sure and universally accepted: It was all the fault of the English, and always had been.

At heart these were ordinary people, pained by royal decrees, unsettled by all the foreigners who had come and gone in the last hundred years. Whether these foreigners had had good or bad intentions, whether they were English, Russian, French, Belgian, or German . . . the trajectory each of them had chosen had opened the way for doubts and a sense of unease. The mirror they all held up to each other reflected an indecipherable image. It was impossible to reconcile these random, incompatible civilizations. The nationalization of oil provided an opportunity for Iranians to reconfigure them-selves, and each individual strove to find his or her source of inspiration.

And among them was Bahram who, at nineteen, was more handsome than ever: a perfectly sculpted face, dusky skin, piercing eyes under low black eyebrows inherited from Sardar. Black as his thick hair, which he wore swept back, black as the depths of his eyes. He was tall and, thanks to his running, had an athlete's slender body. His suit was from Gholhak's excel-lent tailor, and he wore it well. To keep his shirts white he used the same laundress as the town's aristocrats and prominent fig-ures. He wore dark glasses and ties in solid, sober colors. He had the hands of a prince and, God knows where from, a nat-ural elegance. But what women would remember most about him was his smell. The impassioned smell found on the skin of men of the desert. In fact he had "the backbone of a snake," as they say in Iran of anyone irresistible.

His time at Dar-ul Funun, his diploma, and his success in the university entrance exams helped him overcome his fear. Fear that he would be uprooted from Gholhak and torn away from his reassuring everyday pleasures; fear of entering high society, of being constrained, being a stuffed shirt, losing his freedom and the simplicity of peasant life. He lingered in sick-ness and regressed for months on end, as long as it took for him to accept the change, as if stepping back to leap all the further. Now that his neighborhood showed him respect, that he was recognized as the first Gholhaki to achieve a high school diploma, and everyone knew he was a gifted draftsman and a formidable athlete, he had become the incarnation of dreams of success. The elite that Reza Shah had envisioned; the very young men for whom he had instituted new ideas and introduced modernization, the great Iran, a new Persia. But Bahram respected everyone who played a part in his destiny, except Reza Shah. He felt no respect whatsoever for him, or his successor. He had not experienced the chaos before Reza Shah's time, he had no memory of the days when all women wore chadors and *roubandehs*, he did not realize that he might never have seen the faces of all the young girls he enjoyed watching. In Gholhak a school opened just in time to take him in. And instead of admiring the man who gave them this school, they all admired the school's headmaster; instead of admiring their university, they admired the university professors. Reza Shah told them to think, and think they did. He told them to take their example from the West, and they did. With the subtle difference that Reza Shah saw the broad sweeps of western modernization while the students he sent there absorbed its ideas. And so all they remembered of him were his authoritarian tendencies, like all those fathers who—for their children's own good—made them do things with the threat of terrible punishments, and the children remembered only these terrifying punishments and none of their fathers' good intentions. Children remember who their parents are more readily than what they teach, and Reza Shah was a dictator. So Bahram chose his camp: He opposed the monarchy.

He was all the more convinced in his choice because, since the Shah's victory that summer, Mossadegh had grown more radical. He was distancing himself more and more from the court as well as from the more conservative wing of the National Front and from his religious support. The battle would be fierce, his adversaries had already drawn their knives. Bahram's neutrality was no longer tenable—he had to choose and fight.

"I could have been an out-and-out Communist," he told Darra, "but I'm not thrilled by the Toudeh Party's connections with the Soviet Union. It's almost as if they'd give Iran away, or even their own mothers, if Stalin asked them to."

"Well, then, come to us," Darra said enthusiastically. "Join the Iranian Workers' Party. You know we're the party that communicates best with the youth. Our ideologies are inspired by communism and socialism, we don't denigrate religion, and we don't want to be bankrolled by the Soviets."

"I know," Bahram conceded. "The word 'worker' reminds me of my parents, of hardworking peasants. But what really matters is being loyal to Mossadegh and they're abandoning him one by one, even you are. I've made my decision, I'm going to support Khalil Maleki. I think the split he brought about in the Iranian Workers' Party by continuing to support Mossadegh was a good thing, it has to be done at all costs. I'm going to join the new party he's just set up, the Third Power. It's not Western capitalism or Soviet socialism; it's a new power: the third power. You're walking out on Mossadegh, but we're sticking with him all the way."

A nd so Bahram stepped definitively into the world of men, men of his own era: passionate, uncompromising, brave, self-centered, seductive, authoritarian.

The day after arriving at university, Bahram took a shortcut on his way home; he enjoyed discovering unfamiliar little back roads. He looked at the houses, one old, one modern, side-by-side, reflecting the city itself. On the balcony of a newly constructed building he noticed a large poster of a brightly colored parrot and it suddenly reminded him of Talla, the other Talla, his childhood sweetheart, because her sister's name was Toutti, which means parrot. Memories of another time bubbled up.

I was so happy and carefree. Why do things have to change?, he thought, and he acknowledged nostalgically that if anyone asked him now which girl had meant the most to him, which girl would he never forget, he would indisputably reply: Talla.

A young woman appeared on the balcony with a tiny baby in her arms. It took Bahram a few seconds to recognize Talla. Their eyes met. Did she recognize him? He did not hold her gaze long enough to find out but hurried on his way.

So that's what it was. It wasn't just the picture of the parrot that reminded me of her, I could feel her presence. So she's married and a mother already.

He felt sad and betrayed all over again. Unreasonable as it may seem, he would have preferred Talla never to have married, to have stayed in love with him all her life and then one day, infinitely far in the future, when he had done everything he dreamed of doing in love, they would have met again. That was no longer possible. Something had just ended. Love in all its beauty had gone.

Bahram would not be using that road again, and never again would do for a girl what he succeeded in doing for Talla: working a whole summer to earn enough money to have her photo taken. Never again would he think of stowing apples in his pockets to share them with a girl like Talla . . .

From now on he would describe women with only a few trivial adjectives: beautiful, proud, arrogant, kind, jealous, hysterical. Women would primarily be partners in seduction, the stake in men's desires. They had to know how to attract and resist for the game to last a while. If it went on too long, he would tire of it. If it was too short, it was not interesting. Those who could resist for just the right amount of time were the most desirable, they obsessed him and even sometimes made him unhappy. But even for them he made no exceptions when it came down to it. They were all heading inexorably toward their own downfall. Because this man who seemed so in love, who showered them with praise, lavished them with attention, and offered them such rare passion and such intense desire that every one of them felt she was the most beautiful woman in the world, this handsome, devastatingly attractive man would steal silently away the moment they were conquered, when they finally succumbed, when they thought they had found the love of their lives, when they believed they were heading for the happiest of marriages. Gone, without a backward glance or an explanation. And if one of them should ever insist on a reason for this sudden change, she would be confronted with an impatient, irritable, "You're a nice girl, but I can't give you what you want . . . " Worse still, the easy ones, the kind ones, were not even rewarded with these words. They were treated to a knitting of his brows and a beautiful glowering expression so severe that they could only back away or be burned alive.

Women who cried were annoying, but the ones who needed to talk, to know why, or to give their point of view, they were unbearable. There was no need to try to understand, give explanations, or justify anyone's behavior, the desire was simply no longer there. Who cared what had been said three months earlier, who cared what he might have felt then; what mattered was that the urge had gone and these things can't be forced, can't be made to order. And anyway, why make a scene? There are so many other men and women on this earth, they could both find happiness elsewhere. When the breakup went well, Bahram never thought about the woman again, or only many years later in a nostalgic moment.

In any event, an age-old culture of harems and favorites could not be erased from men's consciousness in the space of a decade simply because Iran had come into the modern age. Even though monogamy was officially widely respected, even though women's rights were praised as a mark of elegance, in a country where the king had had a harem until only thirty years earlier and had been monogamous for just ten years, the true possibilities were far too appealing to be relinquished in real life. And so, like many men, Bahram granted himself the right to seduce a constant succession of women as though he were filling up a money box with all their fine qualities in the hopes that when he broke it open a single perfect woman would step out: his favorite.

It would probably have been the same even without his heartache over Talla. Men like him needed an excuse to justify their actions to themselves and to others. But if his own mother had not been so excessive and exclusive, things might well have been different.

Bahram's mind was open to excellence, culture, learning,

and history, but where women were concerned, his ideas changed little: He would hold the door for them, get the check, give them presents if need be, whip out a nice compliment at the right moment, but little more. He very quickly realized that women really liked him. Lots of them came to him of their own free will, and with the others Bahram gradually grasped that they almost all wanted the same thing and that in most cases a few simple catchphrases did the job perfectly. With those who did not dare make the first move and those who wanted to be pursued, he learned how to break the ice: a look, a smile, then nothing for a little while, a few days' absence, and then a more persistent gaze, a few steps toward her . . . He understood the language of women, the no that meant yes, the furtive looks that betrayed desire, the false goodbyes like the little notes slipped among his things, notes that talked of a breakup but were really a desperate bid for attention. Bahram knew that to win women over he had to make them feel unique, make each of them feel she was more woman than all women put together. Afterward, even if they saw him approach other women, even if he hurt them, they would really struggle to cope without the elixir that flowed from this man's eyes, an elixir that made them feel sublime only to destroy them all the more brutally afterward. In other words, he developed the skill of a hunter.

I t is this Bahram who meets Elaheh, a first-year student of Persian literature. Bahram has a preferred type of woman, a sort of fetish. Of course there are blondes, but they are more of a fantasy; in real life, the girls he likes best have small eyes and long lashes so that when they laugh all you see of their eyes are two dark lines. If they have long hair and wear skirts instead of pants, that is even better. Elaheh is a small, slim young woman with long black hair and big brown eyes. A pleasant face, not an immediately striking one, but one whose unique beauty is revealed on closer inspection.

Elaheh's most distinctive characteristics are her keen mind and remarkable intuitiveness, except when she is caught in the snare of love.

She is descended from a distinguished family. Her father is none other than a prince from the former Qajar dynasty. Granted, there are vast numbers of descendants of the women in the Qajar kings' harems, but the title is still impressive. It is a fact of life that princes are appreciated more once they have fallen from power. Like family jewels or old bottles of wine that have gone musty, they have no saleable value but are still the vestiges of a past that is always perceived as a happier time. This prince married Elaheh's mother out of family duty, in an arranged match. Past forty, he was well beyond marrying age and incapable of settling down for himself, so it was his family that urged him to find a wife. A number of girls from good families were introduced to him, and he chose a beautiful young sixteen-year-old, Freshteh, a shy, attractive, and pure girl. They very soon fell into their allotted roles, he because it pleased him, she because it was her duty.

All wise Iranian women are aware that their husbands may have emotional attachments outside the marital home, attachments they themselves would do better to ignore. Most simply prefer not to know, on condition that their husbands have the elegance to play their part at home. This is usually how these things work in homes where courtesy and decorum are the order of the day. But Elaheh's father conducted his extramarital affairs with no discretion whatsoever. Her mother lived in pain every year of her married life, with no possible means of escape. At the time Iranian women very rarely divorced, and the idea would have been all the more unacceptable because Freshteh's family believed her husband had no major faults: he was not an alcoholic, an addict, or a criminal, he did not beat her, and what was more, he was a cheerful and charming man. Of course everyone knew he had a weakness for women; at receptions he made no attempt to disguise his fawning over them. Elaheh's grandfather occasionally furrowed his brow, deeming him indiscreet, but, well, the man wasn't a rapist, he wasn't putting his hand down women's skirts, so it was nothing serious. In fact, as the years went by, people almost found it endearing, it was so much stronger than him, as soon as he was with one or more reasonably attractive women, his smile changed, his eyes twinkled, and even with the best will in the world he forgot all his duties and commitments.

There was only one thing Freshteh's family held against him: he was a Communist. There was nothing to stop an aristocrat being communist and pro-Soviet. Young Iranians who studied in Germany before World War II had had considerable contact with German Communists and had come home as Communists themselves. Quite a snub to the Shah! Iran had increasingly close ties with Germany and welcomed her most brilliant communist intellectuals. Khalil Maleki said of pre-war Germany, "It's not that we've found Communism, but Communism found us."

Elaheh's father had actually studied in France, and it was in Paris that he met communist students; they were descended from the upper echelons of the bourgeoisie and he from the highest ranks of the aristocracy—a match made in heaven. Paris in the Roaring Twenties—the best years of his life. He treated himself to every possible luxury from women to ideas via wine . . . and emerged a Communist. It was in the bastions of communism that Elaheh's father, Manouchehr Amir-Ebrahim, fully developed his aristocratic contempt for money.

Elaheh's mother could have found consolation in another man's arms; some of her friends did just that. They were high-society women, after all; a woman could go to the cinema like a man, she could even travel in Europe. Some led a flighty life. But Elaheh's mother was a believer and her faith would not allow it. In her family women did not wear the veil; they studied, lived in European style, and did not say the mandatory prayers five times a day. But they were believers, they prayed from time to time and performed acts of charity for the poor. In short, having a relationship with any man but her husband would have destroyed her with remorse. Besides, she loved her husband and she thought that, despite all his affairs, he loved her, too, in his own way. She was his wife and the others were just transient. And she was right about that. Her husband loved her even if he paid her little attention, and he would never leave her. She was his guarantee of everyday happiness. When he came home everything was as it should be, she took care of him and the children, she ran the house, they ate extremely well, and their receptions were dazzling.

From her earliest years, Elaheh had seen her mother cry; it was never ostentatious to attract attention or to elicit pity, but usually done in silence in her bedroom; sometimes it was a few tears shed as she busied herself around the house and stopped halfway through some chore, a residue of emotion from the night before. Elaheh knew her mother cried because of her father, but nothing was ever explained to her. Elaheh started watching her father, following his actions and moves, particularly in public, and when she finally understood, she took to systematically—and anxiously—monitoring him. She would apprehensively appraise the other women at dinners and receptions. Would they catch her father's eye? Which one would he target? And yet now Elaheh still loves her father as much as she does her mother. He is always well dressed, his hair neat, and there is a perennial glint of light in his laughing eyes to soften his distinguished appearance.

Elaheh herself is both drawn to and terrified by men like her father. Bahram is made of the same stuff as him, but is different. He can play several seduction games at once but with much more restraint. Obviously, because a ladies' man has a peculiar need for his women to be aware of each other's existence, he always leaves traces, gives clues, and unless the women are blind they will see them. Bahram cannot help himself but he is not impulsive; when he sees a woman he does not stand with his tongue lolling out like a dog, he never allows his desire to be obvious. Bahram has the patience and contempt of a predator.

She noticed him right at the start of the university semester. With his actor's physique he stood out from the crowd of students. He often wears dark glasses and grey suits. She has been observing him discreetly and has noticed that he watches girls, never walks with his hands in his pockets, is left-handed, and is often with one or two other boys, always the same ones. She even heard him whistling once. She has researched what his name means and discovered that Bahram is the Zoroastrian deity of oaths and promises. She thinks this is a good match for Elaheh, which means goddess. And they have almost the same family name. She has ended up thinking about him every morning when she wakes and every evening before she goes to sleep. She has never thought, "He's too handsome for me," not once. Or, "He looks at girls who are prettier than me" or even, "He looks at girls too much." But nor has she thought, "That's a man for me." Elaheh does not think in these terms, she follows her instincts, which have always failed her in love, invariably throwing her right into the lion's den. Much later in life she would learn to accept that she loved the lion's den.

Bahram has not noticed her before this rainy fall day when he is sitting on the ground floor of the library looking out the window, watching the weather outside. Rain is so rare in Tehran that it is always an enchantment. Bahram cannot take his eyes off the window. He sees a girl come over. They are looking almost directly into each other's eyes and, caught out, she looks away. Bahram does not remember meeting her and cannot understand why she looks disconcerted to see him.

A few days later he sees her again; this time he looks at her a little insistently and she reacts in the same way. Bahram now knows she is interested in him, perhaps more. The next time he smiles at her. Then one day when she is sitting in the library reading, he comes and sits opposite her.

"Hello," he says.

"Hello," Elaheh replies, embarrassed and flustered.

"What's your name?"

As a nicely brought-up girl she should ignore this boy, he is not even in any of her classes, but she settles for saying, "Elaheh."

"What are you studying?"

"Persian literature."

"What year are you in?"

"First year."

Elaheh asks no questions, she already knows everything. She is so overwhelmed by his being there, so near her, she does not even have the presence of mind to pretend.

"What are you reading there?"

"It's about contemporary poetry."

Bahram rests his chin on his hand and looks her in the eye until she blushes. Then he gets to his feet, gives her the sweetest smile in the world, and leaves. In the doorway he turns, looks at her one more time, and thinks to himself that she's cute and definitely a nice person.

He leaves feeling amused but little more than that. In the field of conquests, this seduction comes for free. Particularly as his mind is on other things, a first-year student of foreign languages, Firouzeh: mischievous, arrogant, and, in his view, an absolute beauty.

Even though the girls at university are from families that grant them a degree of freedom, it is crucial for a girl to demonstrate that she respects good behavior or she will not be loved. These girls are virgins, and keeping their virginity until they are married is sacrosanct. The boys would not risk taking their virginity; a kiss, a caress, but little more. Bahram would not try to sleep with anyone at university; taking a girl in his arms and kissing her are the only possible forms of enterprise, and even that is a lot. Later, in artistic and intellectual circles, he will meet divorced women—and some who are married or even still single—who have the audacity to take pleasure in their bodies. But his years spent studying are marked, in an almost mystical way, by this disconnect between love and sexuality which is so typically Iranian. Mostly, unmarried men do not sleep with women at all, or perhaps with prostitutes, or occasionally with a servant or a married woman. Some might keep a girl or woman from a modest background, but these women are rarely also the one they love. They are in love with pure, virginal girls whom they hope to marry or, like Bahram, whom they want to hold in their arms and whose hearts they want to win. That is the very definition of love.

Bahram's friends in Gholhak, who are not lucky enough to

go to university and get to know girls so well, fall in love with girls they see in the street. If they exchange so much as a conspiratorial look they think they are engaged. How often Bahram has to console a heartbroken friend because the girl he is in love with—the one he watches out for as she walks past the end of the street, the one he has never even spoken to, whose voice he has never heard—has just gotten married.

But once you know the rules of the game, its limits and boundaries, it is the same everywhere in the world: trying to be loved in the way you yourself want to be loved, at least once in your life.

Confronted with this forbidden sexuality, with these mostly patriarchal families—some are matriarchal, but they are all authoritarian—and the constant insecurity in their lives, not knowing what fate men have in store for them, what whim will alter their father's behavior, what their future life will be like, what decision will suddenly be reached, what freedoms they may lose, no longer being allowed to see one person, being told to marry another, stopping their studies, no longer wearing skirts . . . confronted with all this, some of these young women have succeeded in securing moments of unchaperoned freedom and have turned the game of seduction into playing with fire. The only territory in which women have power: So long as he wants me but can't have me, I shine, I take pleasure in bringing him to his knees, hoping all the while that this one will prove to be the prince who will deliver me from my prison. The hope expressed in the fables they were told as children. Fables that described a prince coming to free the king's daughter, imprisoned by a giant—and that giant would be their oppressive family or tradition or both. These obstacles were like the seven ordeals that the valiant hero has to overcome before his final battle with the all-powerful being we all identify as the giant. And that being could be male or female because the mothers are no gentler than the fathers. After years of frustration and stolen dreams mothers are more comfortable attributing their misfortunes to other, rival women, to the wrongdoers. So they would rather not have daughters, they would prefer to have sons. Having a daughter means being condemned to watching a rerun of the unchanging fate that is a woman's lot; whereas being mother to a man means living the other side of the story through your son. Having a part of yourself in a man, being loved by your son gives a woman a new kind of power over men through motherhood, even if she has lost it through womanhood.

So Bahram thinks about Firouzeh and Firouzeh thinks about Bahram. Bahram thinks about her, but he does not dream of her; since Talla, no girl has ever made him dream, except for the actresses he sees in films. Meanwhile Firouzeh dreams that Bahram will be her prince.

Having bestowed enough of his searching looks and charming smiles on her, Bahram decides to approach Farouzeh, and waits for her outside one of her seminars. A surprised Firouzeh finds an excuse to break away from her friends and walk alone. Bahram follows at a discreet distance and then comes to join her a little further on with a "hello."

She does not look around.

"May I talk to you?" he persists.

She stops, eyes him up and down, then turns her back on him and sets off again more briskly, but confident that Bahram is still watching her, she is careful about how she moves.

It is early winter, it snowed in Shemiran last night. Bahram walked to the bus stop through the snow this morning. As they drew closer to Tehran the blanket of snow grew thinner and broke up, leaving patches here and there, then it disappeared. From the spot where Firouzeh has just left him, Bahram can see the snowcapped peaks of the mountains. He takes a deep breath of the cold air blowing down from the mountains. Right now he needs consolation. He thinks of Elaheh for a moment and wonders where he might find her; it is six in the evening, most classes are over. He gives up on the idea for today.

He is just heading off down the university's main driveway when a woman's voice calls out to him.

"Hello!" the voice cries. God shows such clemency to men like this, and He alone knows why.

It is already dark and Bahram recognizes Elaheh with the yellow light from the streetlamps giving her smiling face and big, happy eyes a fairy-tale brightness. Elaheh is pleased to see him. Bahram's insistent eye contact in the library the other day reassured her that he likes her. So she walks beside him with the easy, affectionate stride of a woman who is loved. By all appearances she is right, Bahram returns her warm smile. They walk toward the gates of the faculty, and Bahram talks to her gently and very politely. He asks her what classes she had today and where she lives, and she asks him the same questions. Bahram points this out and they both laugh. They are heading in the same direction, Elaheh lives halfway between the faculty and Bahram's house. They take a taxi together, one of the collective taxis that take five passengers. They sit side by side in the front of the car with so little room that their shoulders touch. Elaheh is relaxed, Bahram is friendly and even seems pleased and a little intimidated to be with her.

When they reach Elaheh's destination, instead of saying goodbye and continuing on his way, Bahram alights from the taxi with her. They walk on a little way together, then he says his goodbyes, telling her he will go no farther, it might be awkward for her if they met a relation or neighbor of hers. She accepts this with a smile, thanks him for accompanying her, it was very nice traveling some of the way with him, she is very happy to have done it. She has said too much. Because Bahram seemed shy in the taxi, Elaheh thinks he is not sure he has her consent in this game of love and feels she needs to reassure him. Bahram wonders why he got out of the taxi and is teasingly annoyed with himself for going too far. The last few things Elaheh just said bored him, otherwise this could have been rather nice, but now it's just getting ordinary. He thinks of Firouzeh again. After spending this time with Elaheh, the image of Firouzeh shines all the brighter in his mind's eye, her way of being a woman, so attractive, an enchantress—not that he forgives her for how she behaved this evening.

"I'll get her, I'm sure I will," he thinks emphatically.

On his way home in a taxi he closes his eyes and tries to remember Elaheh's face. He can see its outline but cannot recall the details, the line of her nose or her mouth. Something emanates from her, something that overrides her physical presence. You follow her in your thoughts, with your feelings, and forget to look at her properly. Her appeal is on the inside, not visible to the eye. And this frightens Bahram. When he tries to picture Firouzeh's face, he remembers everything, her lips, her eyes, her neck. With Firouzeh, her outer form is dominant. She herself puts emphasis on every detail of her body, she shows her lips, and wants you to look at her eyes, the shape of her eyes. She is attractive because she is an image, because she is concrete. She is not terrifying because she is not an unknown quantity. Her one and only tactic is to say: I am this body and I won't let you have it, not until I allow you to touch it. Simple, straightforward.

J ust two days later Bahram is walking along the faculty's main driveway on his way home when a woman calls out to say hello to him again. He turns around: This time it is Firouzeh. Bahram's face momentarily registers his surprise, but he immediately brings his feelings under control and returns her greeting while treating her to his most appealing expression. Firouzeh instantly creates a diversion by pointing to the naked trees.

"Don't you think the trees look sad in winter?" she asks in a childish voice, then she stands up straight, sticking out her chest and looking him in the eye as she gives a soft sigh.

Bahram is fascinated, he would like to take her in his arms.

"You're doing me the honor of talking to me this evening," he says.

"I was bored on my own. I usually go home with my girl-friends but I've ended up alone this time. I saw you and thought you'd like it if I went some of the way with you, wouldn't you?"

"Definitely!"

"Where do you live?"

"Gholhak."

"We're heading in the same direction, then," she says, "we'll just have to walk together."

"Unfortunately, I'm not going straight home this evening, I have to go pick something up . . . "

He is lying of course. He wants to make her wait. He has

plenty of time, there's no rush, it's all about the game, nothing but the game. For her, though, time is short, she could be married off at any moment, all it will take is for the right caliber suitor to show up and the game will be over. She is of marriageable age, while young men like Bahram have many years of bachelorhood ahead.

Bahram is pleased, and wonders whether this meeting is a chance occurrence or something she planned. In fact Firouzeh saw him getting into the taxi with Elaheh like a pair of conspirators. It came as a shock. She had been under the impression that Bahram thought about, dreamed about, and lived for her alone. She concluded, quite rightly, that disappointment had driven him to this other girl. She realized she had gone too far and decided to correct her mistake. These players have clear, very logical thought processes. They follow the rules of the game. The game's rules are fairly complex, with specific actions and reactions. And life never kills or destroys the players; at worst it disappoints them. So long as the protagonists are playing the same game, then the balance of power shifts one way or the other, much to their delight. But with people like Elaheh, who approach life viscerally, who are not playing but living life fully and without protection, who never follow a preordained pattern but make it up as they go along, guided by subjectivity, by emotional responses . . . life kills them, it destroys them. Because these people do not stop at another person's façade, they want to get to the depths of them, and we are all reticent or even violent toward anyone who breaks us open to see us from the inside, even if it is done under cover of love. We know they are looking within us for something they have lost somewhere else, we know that in the long run they will simply bemoan the fact that they have found no trace of what they hoped to find, and will leave us emptied of our secrets.

Bahram is happy. Firouzeh is his, he knows it. Let the dance begin.

The next day Bahram goes to see *The Great Sinner* at the movies. Everyone tells him he looks like Gregory Peck, and Firouzeh could be as beautiful as Ava Gardner if she wore the dress from the casino scene.

The country is in turmoil but the movie theaters are still full, Iranian women are still as beautiful, and love can withstand anything.

Bahram is in the library and notices Elaheh coming over to him, looking radiant; she says hello, sits down next to him, and gives him a booklet she promised him. Elaheh's father came across something even better than Communism in France: Louis Aragon. And for some time now he has spent his nights in the torment peculiar to those who choose to translate poetry; his specific affliction is a collection of twenty-one poems called *Elsa's Eyes*.

Elaheh mentioned this to Bahram in the taxi and promised to copy out some of the translated poems for him. She has now done this, unbeknown to her father. Bahram has forgotten about the poems and takes a while to remember. He thanks her unenthusiastically and gets up to leave, inventing the excuse of a class about to start. The truth is he wants to find Firouzeh. He feels that four days without seeing each other should have been enough to whip things up a bit. Elaheh is rather disappointed, she was expecting more than this. A date perhaps, or for him to offer to see her home this evening. She would like to interpret this failure of initiative as shyness, as a lack of courage. She tells herself she should have done something, she should be the one to make the first move. He'll never dare. Next time she'll do it. She has a strong urge to delude herself on the subject of Bahram.

God never spares these women any pain, and He alone knows why. On her way out of the library Elaheh sees Bahram and Firouzeh chatting. She sees them in profile and notices that Firouzeh has her head held high and is looking Bahram directly in the eye. Bahram is telling Firouzeh that in *The Great Sinner* Ava Gardner reminded him of her. He prepared all his lines the day before. Perhaps they could go and see it together?

Firouzeh laughs out loud.

"Is that all you want? Do you know who I am? My father's a congressman, I really can't parade myself through the streets with you!"

"As you wish, but have you considered that your father might be proud for you to be seen with me? Do you know that I draw? I'd like to show you my drawings, perhaps one day you'll let me draw your portrait?"

Firouzeh smiles, she is flattered and she likes this young man more by the minute.

"I'll think about it," she says but what she is actually thinking is, He's so handsome, I wish I could marry him. I need to know which family he's from and what his father does.

If she only knew who my father is, Bahram thinks as he watches her walk away, but he quickly banishes the thought. He is in a hurry to find himself a job and some standing, to distance himself from his background, which is a nuisance for him here, at university. In Gholhak he is in his element, people know him, know everything about him, they are all proud of him. Back home he raised himself high enough to look down on people. Here he has to introduce himself, talk about his family and his father's job to people who mostly come from high society. However much he persuades himself that he has a certain standing because of his grades, his talents, and his looks, he knows he will never marry one of these girls. To avoid this painful idea, he tells himself he would rather marry a girl from his own circles, a girl who would not go to university and would be proud of who he is. He'll choose a very beautiful girl and he'll give her dresses her father could never afford, and they'll go to the movies together. She'll take his arm as they climb the steps, everyone will look at them and mistake them for Gregory Peck and Ava Gardner. It will happen, he has plenty of time. It's like the one hundred meters, once he starts running he knows he'll finish it and finish it well.

So Elaheh sees Bahram talking to Firouzeh. Something about the scene indicates a shared interest, something tells her this didn't just start today. Her heart starts beating and her hands shake. Ever since she was a child her hands have shaken when she experiences strong emotions, it irritates her father but other people find it touching. She does not stay to watch them, their complicity is unbearable. She walks away without a backward glance. Elaheh is an attractive young woman, not for her physical beauty but for her energy, her genuine commitment to things in life, and her emotional responses to them, but right now she feels ugly and colorless. Elaheh lacks Firouzeh's narcissism, which would allow her not to need other people's approval to appreciate her own qualities. Firouzeh's ego can be bruised by another person's indifference but she never reevaluates herself, it is always the others who are at fault. Elaheh has a deep-seated need for the mirror other people hold up to her. The reflection she sees of herself in their eyes is vital to her, and right now the mirror is telling her she is ugly. As she walks away from Bahram her footsteps change, they become heavier and her head droops between her shoulders. The same people who might have noticed her a few moments earlier will not see her now. She becomes transparent and disappears.

When she arrives home, Elaheh has a terrible thought. What if Bahram wrote Firouzeh a love letter, and what if in that letter he copied out the poems she handed to him today . . . She was so stupid! She shuts herself in her bedroom and starts to write Bahram a letter. Is she really writing to him? What she says goes beyond this evening's incident, she talks as if she knows Bahram's very soul, as if she knows what

will happen next, as if a year has gone by and a thousand things
have happened. She writes about how this story will end,
before it has even started. Obviously Bahram will not understand because as far as he is concerned there has been nothing
between them. But Elaheh knows exactly what would happen,
she has seen the performance a hundred times, with different
actors, in different settings, and the result is always the same.
At least that is what she believes.

She cries as she writes, but she is not writing in a spirit of
renunciation. She is actually telling Bahram: I know what you're
doing, I know what's going to happen, I know you're going to
cause pain, to me and the other girl, I know you'll cause yourself pain. too, I know that if you carry on like this you'll never
know the love and happiness of being with someone, I'm not
talking about the moment of conquest but what comes afterward, all the years you can spend with another person.

It is a magnificent letter, powerful and full of love. But what
Elaheh does not realize is that men like Bahram have no need
for the love she describes, quite the opposite—a mother's over-
bearing love is enough for a whole lifetime. A woman in love is
suffocating. Bahram needs distance and diversity. That is how
he protects himself from a woman's invasive presence. Even
though paradoxically he constantly needs a woman's presence.
Alluring and repellent, that is how it is. It is this paradox that
makes him difficult to understand, and not the other way
around. It is life itself that makes men like him incoherent. But
Elaheh does not grasp this. She cannot see that these are the
irreversible consequences of a life that is no better or worse
than any other, that turned out this way rather than any other
way, and it would have taken so little for it to be different but
that is not what happened. And she thinks she wants to change
Bahram, but what she is really doing with this letter is asking
life for compensation, it is her own story she wants to change.
She wishes she could forgive her father and make her mother

happy again. Even if a man gave her all the love she longs for, he could not satisfy this need. She would have to succeed in changing a man in the same mold as her father to show that it is possible. This might have been achievable if she did not carry so much resentment around with her. It stops her from taking things slowly; she is instantly stung and she overreacts. She has such striking premonitions of the future and all the events to come, and she reacts in anticipation of tomorrows that do not yet exist.

The following Saturday the whole city is covered in a thick blanket of snow, and Elaheh is sitting on the bench at the university gates waiting for Bahram. He devoted the whole of Friday to politics, at home with his local friends. When he joined the newly formed Third Power Party at the beginning of the fall, the party had no office in his neighborhood, so he gave them the use of a room in his brand-new house. In the summer his parents bought him a small semi-detached house and integrated it into their property. Sardar and Talla still live in their modest two-room house; Talla still wears the same dresses and the same worn shoes, Sardar still has the same patched jacket, and that will never change. But they are growing rich, even though no outward signs betray that fact. Sardar has bought land for a song in small plots all around Gholhak but also on other parts of the Shemiran plains, it was land no one wanted because no crop could be sown on it, but these plots are becoming very valuable. More and more beautiful villas are being built in Shemiran; agricultural land and even the land on the great sterile plains is now much in demand. Sardar did not buy his plots as a speculator, thinking they would one day be worth a fortune. He bought them precisely because they cost nothing, they were all he could afford. And they meant he could feel proud in front of Talla, because he now owned more than he had in Ghamsar. He took pleasure in owning them, but no more than a child who enjoys building a tower of paper, knowing it is only make-believe. In the end, though, and to his great surprise, the tower of paper turned into a castle of stone. Sardar now owns many plots worth a great deal of money. No one knows exactly how much, but a substantial amount.

Talla knows Sardar has bought plots of land, but has no idea where or how large they are. She knows only the exact number of purchase certificates and where Sardar keeps them, just in case he suddenly leaves this world. And Bahram knows nothing about them for now. They do not tell him because he is too young and might be tempted by the devil. But the entire fortune is set aside for him.

So they bought a house for their student son to give him his independence, and to give him the freedom to invite friends over. And Bahram hosts the party's meetings in his new house. The same people who, as boys, liked to come to Bahram's house to dip their fingers into Talla's pots of cream or to gorge themselves on Sardar's watermelons now enjoy coming back to this same garden, this time intoxicating themselves with ideologies. They are continuing their journey together. Except for Darra, who is not from this neighborhood and has not followed in their footsteps. He has stayed in the Iranian Workers' Party and abandoned Mossadegh. But they are still friends. They often argue, sometimes screaming at each other, but the connection between them, which was forged in politics, now reaches beyond that. Each gets from the other something he himself does not have. Darra wishes he had the same presence as Bahram, and Bahram likes going to Darra's house, a traditional bourgeois home with its rules and fine manners, and his warm, courteous, cultivated parents.

Elaheh sits on the bench in her black coat with her hair loose over her shoulders, her face red with cold and anger, gazing into space. As soon as she sees Bahram, she gets up, goes over to him, says a curt hello, and hands him the letter. Bahram is amazed, hesitates before taking it. But Elaheh does not back down, she holds the letter out until he takes it, then leaves. Embarrassed, Bahram looks around, the entrance is swarming with students, some saw the exchange. He blinks as he always does, slips the letter inside a book, and continues on his way. He has not thought about Elaheh for a single second since they met in the library, and he feels he must have missed something. It reminds him of Mahine's letter during Varamine's *Ashura*. He tells himself this time there shouldn't be any posse coming after him to frighten him off, even though the two incidents are separated by only a short time and very little geographical distance. And he laughs about this privately.

He waits until after dinner that evening to open Elaheh's letter, ten pages of it. He reads it in one sitting. Bahram cannot bear being criticized. He reads faster and faster, he wants it to be over, but he simply cannot give up on a letter addressed to him by a girl, even though the tone of voice is uncomfortable for him. A woman who writes ten pages to you, even if they are full of criticism, is basically writing a love letter. When he has finished reading, he folds the pages and puts them back in the envelope. He can feel the power of her words, and the sheer energy of her feelings sets his cheeks ablaze, but not his heart. Elaheh has never mattered to him. He does not even try to remember catching her eye in the library, or the trip in the taxi; these things meant nothing to him at the time, so they mean nothing now. Elaheh should never have gone so far, analyzing details so minutely and reaching the conclusion that he will never experience the deep things in life if he carries on like this. Yes, let's talk about the deep things in life! They're not here, they're in the history books and geography books he learns by heart every evening, they're in those men-only evenings when they discuss all the ideas in the world, they're in the hands of master painters who create divine works of art, and they're certainly not in a woman's guts!

And yet this letter is written in brilliant, formal Persian. In a pinch Bahram might think the girl is extraordinary, but he would rather view this letter as a sort of performance rather than acknowledging its intelligence and its still more remarkable perspicacity. All the same, he feels a certain tenderness for Elaheh. He knows that, despite all the things she wrote to him, it would take only a few words to reverse everything in her mind. But he won't be doing that because she's not the one he wants. He wants Ava Gardner, he wants Firouzeh. And he wants her not for any particular reason, not for anything important. He wants her because she is beautiful and because she takes no interest in his soul. Firouzeh is interested in herself and in what she wants, and Bahram is one of the things she wants, he knows that. Bahram also knows that if you could weigh up honesty, Elaheh would be much heavier. But that isn't important, this isn't some world full of angels, it's a land of men, and all that counts is the sublime beauty of a conqueror's perfect actions. The only mind-blowing, intoxicating thing here is the conquest. No other qualities matter.

Elaheh is the defeated party. She has revealed herself, laid herself bare; with one gesture she showed all her strengths and weaknesses. She has no more surprises for him now.

A few days later Bahram comes across Elaheh and gives her a kindly nod of the head but no more.

It so happens that this same day Firouzeh has invited him to her birthday party. She gave him an invitation card.

What's a birthday party?, Bahram wonders, he has never heard of one—where he comes from people do not even know their birth date. But Firouzeh has studied at a French school and has been celebrating her birthday since she was a little girl. Bahram does some research. One of his university friends also studied at Saint-Louis, Tehran's French school, but what he says does not make things much clearer for Bahram:

"Well, my friend, you had to start sooner or later, but you could have started more gently. You'll have to stick this out now!" he says mischievously.

The party is held in one of the Elahieh gardens not far from where Bahram lives. On the well-founded advice of the same friend, Bahram arrives with a bouquet of roses. Firouzeh is wearing an Ava Gardner dress and he is dazzled. Not only by Firouzeh but also by the lights around the swimming pool that he can see through one of the bay windows. Where should he start? By taking a glass from the tray offered by the white-gloved servant and tasting this bitter, acidic drink they call champagne? Or watching men kiss Firouzeh's hand while holding their cigars poised in their other hands? Or watching the couples dancing swing to the music played by a jazz band?

Firouzeh is in her element. She is radiant, she is *the* woman.

The woman for all these men, all these men paying her so much attention, she does not neglect a single one of them. This is not malicious or fickle, she owes it to herself and to each of them. It is almost a duty. You have to be nice to the people who value you as highly as you would like to be valued. And accept as a compliment the fact that they may not realize there could be a more fragile soul among them who could snap like the stems of the beautiful flowers she is throwing at them right now.

But she is particularly keen to introduce Bahram to her father, the congressman.

"Father, I'd like to introduce my friend from university, Bahram Amir . . . "

"Amir . . . "

A misleading name: short, noble, universal, and it means "sovereign."

"Are you from the Amir family descended from a grandson of Naser al-Din Shah? Or is it Mozaffar al-Din Shah, I don't remember?"

"No, sir."

"I believe there's an Amir family descended from one of the khans in Khorasan," says a man standing next to Firouzeh's father.

"No, sir, my family is from Kashan."

It would be inappropriate to mention Ghamsar.

"There are a good many Kashanis among the Bazaaris, worthy tradesmen," Firouzeh's father forces himself to say, just to please his daughter, but he is thinking, I must tell the girl not to mix with these social-climbing street vendors.

Whatever happens I must avoid the fateful What-does-your-father-do question, thinks Bahram. And he thinks it so hard that a guardian angel hears him: The Shah's younger brother arrives in person and attracts everyone's attention.

Bahram knows he needs to leave before he is asked to dance

or do anything else. He gives the excuse that his mother is unwell, but Firouzeh turns on the charm to get him to stay at least until her cake arrives.

"It would be rude to leave before that," someone says.

So he stays and now here comes the cake with its eighteen flickering candles. He will see plenty more and in a few years' time he will even have forgotten where and when it all started. For now, though, he is enchanted by the sight of his Ava Gardner blowing out her candles . . .

He walks out of that garden in the same state as when he left the Germans all those years ago, except that this time he does not want to go back anytime soon. But he is happy finally to have seen what goes on behind the walls and closed doors of noblemen's gardens, and to have witnessed a Garden Party—the great enigma of his childhood.

Lying in bed that night he keeps telling himself he's a socialist and really doesn't belong anywhere that the Shah's brother might be . . . and he has erotic dreams.

T he following week, Firouzeh agrees to go to the movies with Bahram to see *The Great Sinner*, then lets him steal a kiss from the corner of her mouth. Bahram stays vague about his family, and Firouzeh gradually succumbs to his charm, then falls completely in love while Bahram grows increasingly detached. She now lets him take her properly in his arms, kiss her on the mouth for a long time, and stroke her body, but without ever undressing her completely. He might unbutton her blouse, slip his hand over her breasts, one after the other, run his hand down to her waist and stroke her hips. A triumphant moment of pleasure he will remember for a long time. He will go no farther, but will keep making the same moves until he is sated. Meanwhile Elaheh has done a lot of crying; she waited a long while for a reply to her letter and wrote him several more that she will never send, but she will not forget him.

Then Firouzeh unbuttons her dress herself. Infuriated, Bahram does not touch her. He has tired of these constantly repeated performance. She realizes she has embarked on a love affair that can go nowhere and decides to break up with Bahram. She does it without anger or hatred, saying simply, "We're not made for each other, we'd better stop now, I still like you but this isn't what I want." Saving face is what matters most. She is leaving him before he does the same to her, playing the more pleasing role and walking away from this relationship with her head held high. Her restraint is remarkable.

Bahram is very sorry, he would have preferred a more tragic ending: Firouzeh's parents forcing her to marry someone else and Firouzeh weeping in his arms for days on end.

At the start of spring Bahram comes across Elaheh at the bus stop.

"... I know that you know that I know," he says awkwardly.

"And I know that you knew. You knew exactly what I wanted and you didn't want to give it to me, but you didn't withhold it either. Pretty exhilarating for you. Unconsciously, though, because the image you have of yourself wouldn't let you be conscious of it, and not just where I'm concerned. There must be other women, more fish in the sea. Listen, Bahram, I'm telling you this completely sincerely, you've got lost in your love life, lost between a thousand longings and doubts, not being able to cope without one particular girl but not really wanting any of them, resenting them all ... It's your life, you're master of it, but I can't stay and watch this ... I know you're not interested in what I'm saying, you're somewhere else, wrapped up in different games, but that doesn't really matter. I'm saying it for my own sake, not for yours. By saying it to you I'm actually setting myself free. What I'm about to say may be pretentious, but what the heck, I think I was one of the best things that could have happened to you and you couldn't see it ... "

She blurts all this out without stopping then as she steps on the bus she adds, "Could you take the next bus, please."

Bahram laughs out loud, he hasn't understood a single word. What on earth is she talking about? Why the hell are women so fond of the illusory world of the truth? And why are men so unreasonable?

He gets onto the bus. He has just suffered Firouzeh's last goodbye, he needs comforting.

It really does take very few words from him . . .

From that day on Bahram and Elaheh see each other regularly. She even goes to his little house and they shut themselves away to talk politics and literature. Bahram's background does not shock her, in fact it is a pleasant surprise. Out of loyalty to her father, Elaheh thinks of herself as a Communist. So what more could she hope for to demonstrate her convictions?

She even ends up alone with Talla and Sardar one day. After the other Talla, Bahram's childhood sweetheart, this is the first time Bahram has brought a girl home. And it is her third time here, Talla has been counting, so it must be serious. Talla and Sardar never suspect that Bahram may not bring home the girls who mean something to him because he is ashamed of them, his parents. Sardar is so happy he goes to find a sheep and sacrifices it in front of Elaheh. He slits the sheep's throat in the middle of the yard. He is convinced Elaheh is his future daughter-in-law, she must be welcomed into the family with generosity worthy of her charms. And Talla is not even jealous, she cannot be, Elaheh is from a world to which she has been submissive all her life. You can tell at a single glance, appearances never lie about this.

Bahram enjoys Elaheh's company. No one knows her in Gholhak so they are free to go for walks together in peace through the streets and gardens . . . Bahram has tried to kiss her once under the mulberry tree but she refused. He tried to take her in his arms in his room, she pushed him away.

"This is friendship, we agreed on that," she says.

Bahram does not remember agreeing on anything, but it doesn't matter, they're having fun. He finds her company more and more agreeable, life feels easy with her, there's nothing to hide, nothing to prove. But at the back of his mind he still thinks she is not the one he wants to be seen with later. He would rather walk about in public with a Hollywood beauty, and he would sacrifice every moment spent with Elaheh to achieve that.

Elaheh herself wants much more. She wants the apocalypse and the rebirth. She wants him to go down on his knees before her, she wants regrets—no, more than that—repentance, recognition that he has done wrong, a promise he will mend his ways . . . And she is convinced it is possible, it will happen in the end.

V
ELAHEH,
GODDESS OF SHIPWRECKED SOULS

Ali Farhang is the lecturer Bahram most admires, his master, a Mossadeghist and an eminent teacher, a brilliant orator whose words fill Bahram with passion in the university's big amphitheater, as he talks without notes about the Persians, the Greeks, and the Romans; he has given Bahram a lifelong love of rhetoric and he makes Bahram think "I want to be like him . . . " And this is the man who deducts ten marks from Bahram's end-of-year grade because he arrived late for one of his lessons, accompanied by a new student, a girl who suddenly appeared on the course like an angel sent from heaven, the girl with the golden hair.

Two months before the end of the academic year, Bahram met a new female student. She is the daughter of an embassy attaché who has come home to Iran. She started her university education abroad and has transferred to Tehran University. Her mother is Dutch. She has blue eyes and golden hair.

Perhaps the lecturer is jealous because one of his best students spends time with the girl he himself would so like to have a dalliance with. Just a dalliance. And it makes him behave unfairly, he is abusing his position. Perhaps he thinks his students should be at their most reverential with him and never dare compare themselves to him. Piqued, he lops ten points from Bahram's grade, putting him second in his year group. And at the same time he withdraws his authorization for Bahram to be absent for athletics selections. They will never forgive each other.

On the day of the athletics trials, Farhang has arranged a trip to the Museum of Iranian Antiquities. Bahram keeps looking at his watch and Farhang talks on and on about all these artifacts collected by the museum, although for once he is not really interested in them. If Bahram's permission for leave had not been withdrawn he would already be at Amdjadieh Stadium for the national athletics team trials. It is one of his life's great ambitions to be a part of this team. It is five o'clock before they get out of the museum and are free to go home. Bahram is already running, still hoping something has delayed the selection process, which was meant to take place at two. The gods can't abandon him now, he's trained so hard, he's an excellent sprinter, worthy of the Olympics. He promises the gods that if he is selected for the national team, he will give his best. He keeps making this promise all the way there . . . Iranians really do believe in miracles.

When he arrives at Amdjadieh he keeps running until he reaches the athletics track. The place is empty, everyone has gone, the team has been selected. Bahram collapses to his knees. He weeps with exhaustion and disappointment, alone, in an empty stadium, after dark . . . What could be crueler?

Maybe the absurd thing about this situation is that I still keep talking to you. I still feel like it from time to time, and the way you distance yourself from me doesn't put me off . . . I probably need to tell you these things in order to hear them myself.

I do realize there will always be some girl who's prettier than me and that that's enough to make you to change tack immediately . . . I accept that. And by accepting it, I can't find anything you do hurtful anymore.

I'm not writing to ask you to apologize, there's no need for that; at some point, while I hoped your fire burned with a cold flame, I had my wings burned.

And I want you to know that, right at the start, I trusted you, but then I stopped trusting you. Now that I no longer see myself as a part of your love life, or I should say that I no longer see you as part of my love life, I trust you again. I know people can put their faith in you as a person, even if they can't as a boyfriend.

I see so much in you, some very good, some less so, I see your strengths and weaknesses, but I won't talk about them anymore because there's no point. Because you take that as an attack, and instead of seeing me as an ally precisely because I'm prepared to talk to you about them, you give me the cold shoulder . . .

You are a man in the making, you're too young. Maybe later we'll meet up again on different terms and maybe then you'll be ready to listen to me . . .

Meantime, we don't have to hate each other just because we didn't manage to make something of our relationship . . . If possible, I'd rather we didn't end on a bitter note. I don't know about you, but I'd rather have an image of you that will be a pleasure to look back on. And I'd like it to be the same for you . . . You've made your mark on my life and I'm sure I've made an impression on yours . . . let's see it like that . . .

Lastly, and this is the main reason I'm writing, so you hear it from me and not from anyone else: I've decided to get married. To a man a lot older than me but who will be a loving husband, I'm sure of that.

I don't have anything else to add for now. Maybe I'll keep writing you for a while, or maybe not, and things will fade away of their own accord.

Bahram reads this last letter from Elaheh with tender feelings but no regrets. He feels tired of everything that is happening to him, and thinks life should cut him some slack.

Elaheh marries a friend of her father's, a man twenty years

her senior, Sadegh Mohajer, a journalist and member of the Toudeh Party, so he, too, is a Communist. He asked for her hand in the winter but she turned him down. Then she asked for him to be contacted again and gave her consent.

The marriage takes place in the first month of summer, on *Tir* 15th, in her grandfather's summer residence in Darband, at the foot of the eternal mountain, a place that sees the family come and go from generation to generation, immutable, untouched by pain, regrets, or love. The bride in her white dress cries after saying, "I do," which is normal, the bride always cries, so does her mother. Everyone in Iran cries, with happiness and in sorrow. People cry so much that they can hide any feelings they like behind other, more acceptable emotions. This bride cries because she does not love her husband and she loves someone else, but that happens so often here that even the angels pay no attention. What also often happens is that two weeks later the same girls end up in love with their husbands, if they know how to treat their wives properly, unlike the other men who have broken their hearts.

Elaheh's husband always calls her Madame, he speaks to her and treats her with the utmost respect, kissing her hand and reminding her of her freedom and her rights, saying, "It's up to you" and, "That's for you to decide" . . . and she ends up loving him. Especially afterward. After the events that flare up so quickly. Because these are uncertain times, each individual plays out his or her fate on a knife edge, still believing in all its possibilities and taking risks, risking everything, risking life itself. She chose a member of the Toudeh Party because Bahram does not like the party. She chose a proper rival for him. A monarchist would have been ridiculous, Bahram would have laughed in her face, but a Toudeh Party Communist—and what is more, no ordinary Communist, an important journalist, a well-read, cultivated, and committed man—makes a perfect rival. She hopes Bahram will hate him with a loathing that will consume him for the rest of his life. But calculations in love are always wrong.

When Bahram is told her husband's name by a friend, he says, "No, really? Goodness! That's great, that's great! He's a good man. I've read his articles, I think he studied in France. That's fantastic!" And no more.

Men are jealous only if they were in love, otherwise a former girlfriend's marriage is comforting, especially if he treated her tactlessly and if she is marrying a good man. It's fantastic.

Then the day came, *Mordad* 28th. Through history some events endure forever, a past that still exists in the present, a shipwreck that still floats over the ocean—haunting, obsessive. Because fate takes a course that leads to the Apocalypse when there was clearly another possible path. People refuse to accept that these events are truly over, and they doggedly ponder, study, and write thousands of words in an effort to find one detail to shed some light on why these things happened, even though the events themselves are not worthy of those who suffered them, nor those who committed them: the Mongol invasion, *Mordad* 28th, 1332 . . .

The Shah and his queen had already fled abroad after an attempted coup against Mossadegh, which was thwarted thanks to the network of Communist officers in the Toudeh Party. On *Mordad* 26th the National Front and the Communist Party both organized huge demonstrations in Tehran, and the Communists toppled statues of the Shah and his father.

On *Mordad* 27th, Mossadegh met the American ambassador, who expressed his concerns about the increasing Communist presence in Iran—the Americans hated the Communists and were afraid Iran might side with the Soviets. Everything else, even oil, was only a secondary consideration. That same day Mossadegh asked Iranians to stop demonstrating in the street, he wanted to restore order.

Tehran's public squares emptied, now they simply needed occupying. That was when American agents gave the order for a coup. The operation was codenamed AJAX and was run from Tehran itself by the nephew of former U.S. president Franklin D. Roosevelt. And Mossadegh could not believe the Americans would do something so scurrilous.

At siesta time you can barely even hear the buzz of flies, it is immediately swallowed by the silence that watches over Gholhak's sleeping inhabitants.

Toward two in the afternoon there are suddenly three knocks at the door. Without waiting to be invited in, Ebrahim rushes into the garden.

"Bahram! Bahram!"

"I'm coming," Bahram calls from his house.

"Hurry up," Ebrahim keeps yelling.

He runs past Sardar, who was taking his siesta in the garden under the mulberry tree and who has just woken with a start, but Ebrahim does not even say hello.

"The worst thing possible may have happened . . . " Sardar hears from some way off, and then Ebrahim whispers in Bahram's ear . . .

"I'm going out!" Bahram shouts. When he is at the garden door he can just hear his mother's voice but does not listen.

Sardar understands, he gets up and switches on the radio.

"What are you doing? This is no time to listen to the radio!" Talla exclaims, surprised. Sardar does not reply and something stops Talla from pressing him further. Knowing Sardar, this must be serious.

As soon as they are in the street the two young men part with a "see you later." Bahram starts running toward Tehran; his job is to go check that the rumors circulating in Gholhak are true.

Bahram is now twenty and he runs through Gholhak's streets with ease like a Greek god, light, swift, and supple. When he reaches Shermiran Road he takes a taxi into Tehran. The taxi draws near the capital and even from some way off there is a sense of the chaos in the city center. Pedestrians run in every direction, a crowd gathers, men armed with sticks and knives appear, soldiers arrive, there are shouts and groans. The taxi driver can go no farther so Bahram alights and melts into the crowd. A dark mass of people crying, "Long live the Shah! Down with the traitor Mossadegh!"

"Please, please, what's going on?" Bahram asks.

But no one gives him a clear answer, as if what is going on has not yet fully happened, it is too soon to give it a name. He needs to know. He elbows his way to the Bahar Café on Shah Avenue. The manager, Jamshid Khan, is an active party member. Bahram comes here often for student meetings, to drop off tracts and have a beer. Khan is an unusual man, an Azari who speaks Persian with a strong Turkish accent; he must be about fifty or older, hard to tell. He has the moustache and bulk of a Turk, a genuine smile, and big, kindly hands. He always knows everything that is happening, has friends everywhere, a network of informers; he knows the news even before the newspapers publish it. No one knows exactly where he is from and a lot of stories are told about him, but one thing is almost certainly true: He was once a member of the Toudeh Party and now no longer is. At least that is what his words imply, but he does not state this clearly. He will be able to tell Bahram what is going on. If the café is open.

The metal shutter has not been lowered, but the café is empty and the door locked. Through the window, Bahram can see the key in the lock, and someone hovering inside. He is about to knock when he sees Taghi, the waiter, coming to the door. Taghi was on the lookout at the back of the café and recognized Bahram. Jamshid Kahn told him to open the door only to party members he knows well. He lets Bahram in and goes to tell Jamshid Khan.

"Come through to the kitchen," Taghi says.

Jamshid Khan has his back turned, he is standing by the oven burning papers. Bahram feels sick with impatience.

"Ask Taghi to serve you some tea," Jamshid Khan says without turning around, "and come sit next to me here."

"Please tell me what's going on!"

"Do as I ask."

Tea in hand, Bahram sits down next to Jamshid Khan, who is still calmly and carefully dropping papers into the flames one by one. As if defeat has become familiar to him, as if he wants to act out this part as appropriately as every other, he wants the beauty of his gestures to show that there is no end goal, all that matters is the road you take, and that road leads from one disaster to the next. As if he once met Talla's aunt Gohar, and she told him, "Man is revealed in defeat . . . You'll see, every time you do your duty as a man, defeat will be there. You might as well love it and cherish it. Drink it like tea that is as bitter as poison the first time but afterward, if you accept it, it will reveal you to yourself."

"If you knew how many times I've done this in my life," Jamshid Khan says with a sad smile. "It started early this morning, at about eight, a load of people, thousands, thugs from the south of the city, armed with sticks and knives, hired hands shouting, 'Long live the Shah!' and 'Death to Mossadegh!' And the best of it is the chief of police ordered his forces not to move, to leave them to it! They went to the bazaar and the *bazaaris* shut up their shops. Then there were more and more of them. Do you know what? Buses full to bursting came from God knows which suburb and since then the buses have been driving all over town bringing more people to the demonstrations. We don't know where they're from or who paid the drivers. They've already ransacked the offices of the political parties, and ours, too. The Toudeh Party's premises have been completely destroyed . . . And the offices of at least twenty newspapers, some are on fire! They've also taken the army headquarters. And they've freed Shaban the Brainless from prison, he's the ringleader of the street fighters bankrolled by the royal court, and he's already out in the streets leading his troops. Does that give you some idea how highly connected these bastards are? They've also captured the radio station, General Zahedi has already made a speech announcing that the Shah's appointed him as the new prime minister. Right now these lowlifes are launching an attack on Mossadegh's house, his guards are holding out for now . . . "

The telephone rings. Jamshid Khan leaves the kitchen but comes straight back.

"It's over," he says. "Army tanks are crushing Mossadegh's house as we speak. They've got their coup. Sometimes it works, sometimes it doesn't. It didn't work last week . . . but this time it has."

Jamshid Khan starts talking very quickly, his hands jittery. "Now listen up, go home straightaway, don't stop anywhere, don't talk to anyone. When you're home clean everything out, don't leave a single piece of paper, nothing. Don't trust the little things you're tempted to keep as souvenirs. Then, complete silence. You've never been a member of the party, you've never been to a single party meeting, none of your friends have ever been activists in a party. Even among yourselves you can't talk about it again. Listen to me, from now on no party will or can be tolerated in their eyes, there won't be any political parties. Erase the whole thing from your memory. You'll never come back here, even to drink tea. Now go. Wait, do you have anything in your pockets?"

"I don't think so . . . Oh, yes I do."

"Put it in the fire."

Jamshid Khan takes Bahram in his arms and kisses him on both cheeks.

"Another time, you'll see, another time . . . " he sighs, and this is the first time since Bahram arrived that he has revealed a hint of despondence. Then he smiles and adds, "In a few years, if we're alive, we'll put this together again! Go on, my boy, go. Hey, don't run, walk."

Bahram is worried. He can hear shouts and gunfire in the distance. Tanks roll past him on Shermiran Road. He is jostled by the crowd. Dust everywhere. He feels dizzy, fear sweeps over him, overwhelms him. He cries like a child who has lost his mother. He cries in terror but also with disappointment. Until today this era he lives in belonged to him. He was part of a group, strong, determined men guided by prestigious leaders. These were hugely significant times, and they were heroic. Now, suddenly, he has been robbed of his community. His roots are being cut away from under him. He realizes that his ideals will now be banned, and he will have to forget, to wipe himself from his own memories. All of that was who he was, but no longer can be. He looks around, hoping a familiar face will come to help him, someone will take his hand and lead him to where he needs to go. But no one is interested in him. For a few more minutes he tries without success to find some compassion in the faces bustling around him. Then he instinctively starts running as fast as he can toward Shemiran, as if he is being pursued by armed men, as if his life depends on it. He has to run away from fate. He stops looking at people's faces, does not turn round when he hears cannons boom, he just runs. When he passes through Shemiran Gate, things gradually grow calmer. He has escaped the feverish activity and is now in Shemiran, where time seems suspended, where it has always been possible to stop the clocks and for the pages of newspapers to stay blank, a place where history has never set foot, where only life's everyday things happen. He keeps running on and on, until he sees Shemiran's gardens, its gardens of consolation. Shemiran the maternal, the protector, Shemiran with its enduring fragrance of the peace of paradise. Shemiran is an oriental woman, she never stands up to men but takes them in her arms and soothes them.

When he reaches Gholhak, Bahram slows a little and goes directly to Ebrahim's house. He knocks three times, goes straight in, and lets himself collapse to the floor. Lying there on his back, all he can hear is the frantic beat of his heart. He thinks he might die like the Greek soldier who ran from Marathon, but only after speaking many more words than this historical precedent. He must hold out long enough to pass on the message.

Eyes popping, Ebrahim comes and sits beside him and shouts, "Water, water!"

"There's been a coup, army tanks have destroyed Mossadegh's house, the Shah's back . . . I saw Jamshid Khan," Bahram tells him, and he repeats what Jamshid Khan told him word for word.

Ebrahim helps him back to his feet and leads him to the door, saying, "I'm going out."

As they leave they are obscurely aware of a woman's voice saying something but they ignore it.

Ebrahim's sister is left transfixed under the cherry tree, the glass she offered to Bahram still in her hand. She heard what he said. The two men have left and she is alone in her garden, toward the end of a summer afternoon. The temperature has dropped, her father will come out of the house to do the watering, her mother is frying eggplant for the evening meal, and the crows are cawing.

She looks up at the sky and says, "God, only if you can, only if you want to. Please do it. Tell me it's still possible for the Mossadeghists to win."

Ebrahim runs and Bahram walks. Outside his own front door, fear grips him again: What if they're here waiting to arrest him? But who? He doesn't know. He enters the house cautiously, the radio is murmuring; his mother is hunkered down on the terrace, she says hello to him but he ignores her. He goes straight to the room that he lends to the party, unhooks the large "Third Power" banner from the wall and throws it into a corner, then scoops up the tracts from the table and chucks them onto the banner.

Darra arrives, they look at each other, and Darra glances at the mess.

"Has *your* party cleaned everything out?" Bahram asks him.

Darra is upset, he does not know, he did not have the heart to go look.

"You have to, go see everyone, one by one, you have to clear everything out, burn it all. All of it! Don't keep a thing, not in your pockets, not in any drawers. Nothing. And as of now, none of this ever existed, we'll never talk about it again. Listen to me, no political party can or will be tolerated in their eyes, there won't be any political parties anymore, not yours or mine. Maybe one day we can put this together again, maybe one day . . . I can't make you to do anything, obviously, you do what you like, but don't ever talk to me about it again."

And he turns away to go stack the chairs. Darra leaves, still more frightened than when he arrived. Bahram takes down flags and throws them on the pile too. The portrait of Mossadegh is still there. Bahram stands looking at the photo, hesitating, his hands do not want to take it from the wall.

"Take it down!" Ebrahim says, coming into the room.

Bahram gathers up everything he has put into a pile and goes out, and Ebrahim follows him with the picture of Mossadegh.

"We need to burn everything," he says.

Talla has come to the door and says, "Over there, at the bottom of the garden."

She makes no reproachful comments, is extraordinarily calm, as if aware that this is too serious to make a scene. Bahram turns around and sees her following them with her head lowered. So, my mother does know when to stop . . . he thinks, and that is when he remembers the curse of the cat that meant so much to his mother . . .

Bahram dumps the things he is carrying onto the ground and goes back for everything that is still in the room: books, notepads, newspapers. Talla covers the pile with straw, Ebrahim puts the portrait of Mossadegh onto the straw, and Talla sets it all alight.

Sardar joins them; he has been listening to the radio all day with Talla sitting beside him. They even listened to Tehran radio's historic silence.

All four of them sit around the fire without a word. Talla thinks her son is out of danger now, but she still recites some verses from the Koran.

What times we live in . . . Sardar thinks. That afternoon he heard the announcement about the coup on the radio: "Your attention please, this is Tehran, in a few minutes . . ." What times! Even during the war, under foreign occupation, even our fear of the Russians and the English didn't make us burn anything, in the night like thieves, like enemies of the state. My son's a good man, he's honest, shame on you! But, as usual, he does not say this out loud, he keeps his words locked inside. Except that this time he thinks it openly, for once he is not afraid the Shah might read his thoughts . . .

Bahram's mind is flooded with shame and disappointment. He closes his eyes and pictures Mossadegh's face, and when he opens them he sees that same face burning in his garden. He closes his eyes again and feels Mossadegh stroke his hair with a fatherly hand, before walking away. Bahram would like to go down on his knees before him, to clasp his legs and cry, "No! Don't go! I'm lost without you, we're all lost!" But Mossadegh walks away inexorably.

Bahram remembers the Spartans again, and their motto: "Behind the shield or on it." It occurs to him that right now he is neither behind his shield nor on it, and that this is the definition of shame.

Then he thinks of the foreign minister, Hossein Fatemi, whom he sees as the most noble man on the current political scene. What will happen to him? The Shah despises him. He was first to talk of abolishing the monarchy, and to say that the Shah's court was a hotbed of corruption . . . he has always been ahead of his time: with setting up the National Front, with nationalizing oil . . . "We have governed this country for three years and not killed a single one of our opponents, because we did not come here to kill our brothers. We rebelled in order to make our country unite against the stranglehold of foreigners. And we believed that even though in the past, under terrible pressure, some of our fellow countrymen were influenced by foreigners and obeyed their wishes, they would change when we secured our own sovereignty. But, alas, wolves beget only wolves . . . " Fatemi will say before the firing squad. When Bahram hears of his death he will remember this evening, and will weep as only a man can.

A blank moment, the fire burning, nothing else. Then Bahram remembers the words of his party leader, Khalil

Maleki: "Dr. Mossadegh, the path you have chosen leads to hell, but we will follow you all the way there."

Bahram suddenly thinks of Elaheh and realizes her husband will end up right in middle of that hell. He's had it! A sob makes Bahram shudder. He cries for Elaheh with all his heart. He cries because he has lost her, because she has lost her husband and because everything is lost. Then he thinks of Firouzeh, who is in the winning camp this evening. He can picture her in her Ava Gardner dress, standing in the bay window of her grandfather's house with a glass of champagne in her hand, clinking it happily with other people. And he pictures Elaheh, her eyes full of tears. It's too late now to swap things around. And he keeps on crying with anger, against Elaheh and for her; why do the losers always have to be the most sensitive? And then, spontaneously, he remembers the last verses from the book of Louis Aragon poems that Elaheh gave him:

One fine night the world met its demise
On reefs lit up by the shipwreckers' blaze
But what I saw shining above the sea haze
Were Elsa's eyes, Elsa's eyes, Elsa's eyes.

E brahim goes home. Talla invites Bahram in for supper, but he is not hungry. He goes out, walks through Gholhak's narrow streets for while, with no particular aim. This evening he needs a father, a guide. This evening he feels he does not have the father he would have liked. So he decides to go see Darra's father, Mr. Tabarrok.

It is the maid, Kokab, who lets him in and suggests he wait in the guests' reception room. Bahram declines the invitation, saying he needs to see Mr. Tabarrok only for a moment. Kobab goes off to the living room, and Bahram hears a man's voice calling, "Come in, please." He steps toward the room, and Mr. Tabarrok is already on his feet, coming to greet him. When Bahram comes into the living room he sees Darra along with his older brother Homayoun and their mother. She gestures kindly to Bahram, inviting him to sit down.

He looks at Darra, and can read the distress in his eyes. He knows that Darra now regrets not following him and joining the Third Power because right now Darra is even more ashamed than he, Bahram, is angry: Darra abandoned Mossadegh, but is still going down with him in his disgrace.

Then he looks at Homayoun, who studies medicine in Paris and has come to spend the summer vacation with his family. He is not involved in all this. He has only one goal in life, to qualify as a doctor, a specialist, in France, to take over the consulting rooms from his aging father who is just a general practitioner, and become the uncontested pride of the family. At this moment Bahram envies him, some people are just like that, nothing can ever blow them off course.

Bahram joins the others sitting cross-legged on a mat, and turns to Mr. Tabarrok.

"I went into Tehran. There's been a coup."

"I know."

"The place was in pandemonium. There were men armed with sticks and knives, there were even women with them. Some people were driving around in cars, brandishing their sticks and yelling, 'Death to the traitor Mossadegh!' There were armed police everywhere, all united against Mossadegh. But mostly there were masses of ordinary people, it was as if the whole city was out in the streets, demanding that the Shah be reinstated. But the day before yesterday the whole city was in the streets celebrating the Shah's exile. How's that possible? What's going to happen now?"

"Nothing," Mr. Tabarrok says flatly. "The arrests will start this evening. They'll go hammering on doors, bursting into people's homes, waving their guns, shoving women and children around, and arresting the men. They'll tie their hands behind their backs, grab them around the neck, and bundle them into cars. They'll imprison some and shoot others. No one will say a word and no one will move a muscle. People will go back to their old routines. And nothing else will happen."

"But that's not possible," Bahram retorts fervently. "What about all the parties, and all the people who were out in the streets only yesterday, demonstrating every day for months. They'll be back in the streets, they'll bring the Shah down."

Kokab brings in a tray of tea. They all help themselves. Mr. Tabarrok takes a sugar lump, puts it in his mouth, brings his glass of tea to his mouth, and takes one sip, then another, before eventually breaking the silence.

"Mossadegh made mistakes, too," he says. "Even if everything he wanted to do was fair and needed doing in a perfect world. But he couldn't do everything in such a short span of time, and on his own. They all get it wrong. They're all in such a hurry, too much of a hurry. In a hurry to change everything, change people, change traditions. They're all aristocrats with aristocratic tendencies, noble and arrogant. Good nobility but bad arrogance. They want everything to be the way they see it, they want the best, straightaway. Like in their own homes, where everything comes from the best sources in Iran. They send their servants out specially to buy cheese in Tabriz and cakes in Ispahan. And the same goes for their ideas, their thoughts. Men are sent off to Europe to come back with the best ideas. These people want the best of everything here: the constitution, a secular society, freedom of expression, civil rights . . . Except you can't just place an order for things like that, or buy them; they have to be learned and they take time, a long time. But they want it to happen quickly, to sweep all the religious aspects of public life aside, they want to do it in the space of a few years, in one fell swoop if possible, and this is in a mainly traditionalist country! And when I say mainly, I mean eighty percent illiterate. Take your time, my friends, take your time."

The veins in Mr. Tabarrok's neck are bulging, he is almost shouting. He needs to get it all out this evening. But saying it to his wife and sons would simply have been a husband and father trotting out the same old things again. Bahram is a blessing, God has sent him so that the old man is not stifled by all those words stuck in his throat.

"The worst of it is that, from Reza Shah to Mossadegh, they have the makings of great men, of visionaries. But there's one thing that not one of them will countenance. Do you know why this country will never see a democracy, or freedom? Why we'll always be led by dictators? Whether that's the Shah or someone else . . . " He takes a sip of tea before answering his own question: "Because all our troubles derive from our own weaknesses."

He stops there, says nothing more, as if reflecting on how apt this Persian proverb is.

"If we're to achieve freedom," Homayoun says after a while, "if we're to have national sovereignty and a democracy, there need to be a lot of us who believe in it in our hearts, deep inside our souls."

He says it in a way that implies he already sets himself apart from them.

"Who really believed in it?" Mr. Tabarrok asks, fired up again. "Who? To be honest, of all those who claim they did, there can only be a dozen. The others would all reject an authoritarian regime, but they'll all use force to implement their own ideas. And not one of them took the time to think about the day-to-day realities of Iranians' lives, all Iranians. Take your parents, for example, who's doing anything about their education? They're recognized as illiterate and then what? Don't they see? This country's full of illiterates. Eighty percent! I'm sure that even you're not doing anything about it. You're more ashamed of them than anything else. We're all ashamed of them, because we've broken away from them, from eighty percent of our own country. The only people who still talk to them are the mullahs. And then people complain that religion's too powerful! Even the Communists talk about nothing but the workers in a feudal country! There are so few literate people here that they think they rule the place."

Mr. Tabarrok is no longer really talking to the others, he is staring straight ahead, as if addressing the nation.

"They need to form an alliance with their own people, and the people need to be in alliance with their leaders. The people as they actually are, not as others would like them to be. Mossadegh managed it for a while, he really did. That's why he'll go down in history more than the others. But then where did he go wrong? Ah! I don't want to judge him. Not this evening, anyway."

"But we, the Iranians, we're complicated and difficult to understand," Homayoun says. "When I come back to Iran now I wonder what a foreigner would make of our obsessive good manners, our endless little thoughtful considerations, our terms of affection bandied about the whole time, calling everyone 'my soul,' even some stranger who's just appeared, and saying, 'May I be sacrificed for you,' just as readily to the local grocer as to a child—"

"That's down to our history," Mr. Tabarrok interrupts him. "We learned to lie in order to survive. Probably because the truth is unbearable. Accepting once and for all that the empire no longer exists, and a more powerful force has annihilated Persia, and we can't turn back time, and Cyrus won't rise from his grave and launch his army against the invaders, or march into Babylon—we can't cope with it. So we've told ourselves lies for centuries, and we've become very good at self-deceit. We're lying to ourselves and to others, about our beliefs, ourselves, them . . . We'd rather tell someone else the truth with a knife behind our back. Some become traitors, others just take pleasure in the tragedy. And tragedy is a story that goes on and on. Tragedy won't allow for grief because it keeps rising from its own ashes. Our national emblem should have been a phoenix. We enjoy being part of a personal and collective tragedy, it's theatrical, with endless twists and turns, and we stitch together the same story every day, just using different colored thread, and it's been going on for centuries . . .

"Do you see, my children, we'd like to think we're still the Persians of old, it's like opium, it dulls our pain. So we look away into the distance to avoid seeing what's under our noses.

"I'm not saying we're bad or good. I'm saying we are what we are and ever since Naser al-din Shah we no longer want to be us. We want to be them, but at the same time we hate them because we're not them! We don't realize that we all depend on each other, us and the Greeks, us and the Arabs, the Mongols, the

Turks, the Russians, the Europeans, and the Americans, everyone who's eyed up or occupied our land. Not out of some meaningful connection or mutual respect but to pool our strengths. They can offer their weapons, their schemes, their technology, and modern advances, us with our words, our appeal, and our charm. Oh, we can recite poetry, we can charm our invaders, we celebrate with them, drink their wine, and intoxicate them and, by seducing them, we force them to adopt our customs and that makes us very proud. Then when drunken revelries are over, we weep about the state we're in, and it all starts again the next day.

"They're only that magnificent and that powerful because we make them believe they are, and by making them believe that we make them dependent, and we save our own skins and let ourselves survive respectably. Except that we know and they know that they're the ones holding the sword. That doesn't stop us nibbling away at them slowly from the inside until one day the whole edifice they built up so well on our land collapses. And when it falls we cry tears of guilt. Guilty of admiring and loathing them at the same time.

"And when I say 'we' I mean you and me. I do realize that but I forget it and tend to mean 'we the Iranians.' Because at the end of the day, what do I know about what they want, what all Iranians want? It's just, my son, I say it because when I'm thinking about what Iran really is I also automatically wipe eighty percent of the population from sight. And you do the same. Do you actually know what your father wants? Have you ever once asked him? Have you asked him, 'Father, what do you think about Iran? How do you see its future? If you were in power what would you change?' It's never occurred to you to do that, has it? It never occurred to me either, to ask my old father what he thought about it all. And I don't think it occurred to them to tell us what they thought either. Maybe because they felt nothing needed changing. Maybe they felt life is perfect as it is. How would we know? We never asked them.

"So that's why, my son, this country will never experience peace and freedom in my lifetime nor, I'm sorry to have to say, in yours nor even, I would say, in your children's. What would be the point of freedom when enslavement is so tragic, tragedy is so poetic, and poetry is so Persian!"

His wife is crying, so is Darra. Sitting in the doorway like any good servant, Kokab has drawn her chador around her face and is also weeping silently.

Mr. Tabarrok looks at them affectionately, one after the other, including Kokab, and he thinks, She's Iranian, too, it never occurred to us to ask what she thought about all this either.

And this idea that never occurred to him seems strange. The idea of asking Kokab, his maid, what she thinks of, for example, how Iran is governed. Or, simpler still, what she would change if she were in power. Strange and cruel because he realizes that despite everything he has just said, nothing would make this conversation possible, Kokab herself would refuse to answer, at best she would think he was making fun of her. But mostly he himself would never dare to.

Mr. Tabarrok suddenly finds he is shaking as he looks at Kokab's hidden face. He has just realized that he, too, would be incapable of forming an alliance with Kokab or with people like her. Because he would immediately lose everything he has fought for all his life: distinguishing himself from them. And he acknowledges that, betraying his own words, he, too, has put the knife in his fellow countrymen's back before grasping that he was one of them. What have I said? he thinks.

He smiles and then laughs, and tears roll down his face.

"Do you see, my son? Do you see that *I've* just contributed to it? I've just given you a tragic lecture about our tragedy! Forgive me, my son, for letting you down."

But it is too late. His words have been too powerful, as powerful as the sense of powerlessness washing over him. He will not save them and he will not save himself either from this slow shipwreck that started so long ago.

He now knows that all that is left for him is to pass the time until his edifice—the one built by him and those like him on the land of the illiterate eighty percent he has just been describing—until that edifice collapses.

"There is one thing we can be proud of: We Iranians invented the only two things that give men any consolation for their cruel destiny—paradise and wine! And better than that, couched in our beautiful language, our poets serve them up to us in a single verse! Kokab, go and fetch a bottle of wine and four glasses, and pass me the book of Hafez's poems."

That evening fires were lit one after another in Gholhak's gardens. That evening Gholhak's little streets smelled of burning paper and desperate prayers. Yet the sky was clear and the stars shone. Sardar and Talla sat in their garden, side by side, without a lamp, by the light of the moon. A cool wind brought the smell of jasmine and damp soil; and not a single sound disturbed the familiar silence of Gholhaki nights. Sardar smoked his pipe, Talla poured the tea. There was nothing to bother them that evening, not even their son's absence. Sardar put his hand on Talla's.

"Allahu Akbar! The world is so beautiful here this evening. What more could we ask?"

Parisa Reza was born in Tehran in 1954 to a family of intellectuals and artists, and moved to France at the age of seventeen. She was awarded the Prix Senghor 2015 for her novel, *The Gardens of Consolation*.